the Vampire Diaries

Stefan's Diaries

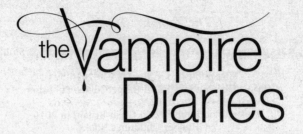

the Vampire Diaries

Stefan's Diaries

volume one
ORIGINS

Based on the novels by
L. J. SMITH

and the TV series developed by
Kevin Williamson and Julie Plec

Hodder
Children's
Books

A division of Hachette Children's Books

First published in the USA in 2010 by
HarperTeen, an imprint of HarperCollins Publishers

This edition published in Great Britain in 2010
by Hodder Children's Books

1

ISBN-13: 978 1 444 90166 5

Typeset in Meridien and Neuland by Avon DataSet Ltd,
Bidford on Avon, Warwickshire

Printed in Great Britain by
Clays Ltd, St Ives plc

The paper and board used in this paperback by Hodder Children's Books are natural recyclable products made from wood grown in sustainable forests. The manufacturing processes conform to the environmental regulations of the country of origin.

Hodder Children's Books
a division of Hachette Children's Books
338 Euston Road, London NW1 3BH
An Hachette UK Company
www.hachette.co.uk

PREFACE

They call it the witching hour, that time in the middle of the night when no humans are awake, when creatures of the night can hear them breathing, smell their blood, watch their dreams unfold. It's the time when the world is ours, when we can hunt, kill, protect.

It's the time when I'm most eager to feed. But I must hold back. Because by holding back, by hunting only those animals whose blood never quickens with desire, whose hearts don't pound with joy, whose yearnings don't make them dream, I can control my destiny. I can hold back from the dark side. I can control my Power.

Which is why, on a night when I can smell blood all around me, when I know that in an instant I could connect to the Power I've been resisting for so long and will resist for all eternity, I need to write. Through writing down my history, seeing various scenes and years connect to each

1

other, like beads on an everlasting chain, I can stay connected to who I was back when I was a human and the only blood I ever heard rushing in my ears and felt pounding in my heart was my own . . .

CHAPTER
1

The day my life changed started out like any other. It was a hot August afternoon in 1864, the weather so oppressive that even the flies stopped swarming around the barn. The servants' children, who usually played wild games and shrieked as they ran from one chore to another, were silent. The air was still, as if holding off on a long-awaited thunderstorm. I'd planned to spend a few hours riding my horse, Mezzanotte, into the cool forest on the edge of Veritas Estate – my family home. I'd packed my satchel with a book and was intent on simply escaping.

That was what I'd been doing most days that summer. I was seventeen and restless, ready neither to join the war alongside my brother nor to have Father teach me to run the estate. Every afternoon, I had the same hope: that several hours of solitude would help me figure out who I was and what I wanted to become. My time at the Boys Academy had ended last spring, and Father had made me hold off on enrolling at the University of Virginia until the war had ended. Since then, I'd been curiously stuck in the in-between. I was no longer a boy, not quite a man, and utterly unsure of what to do with myself.

The worst part was that I had no one to talk to. Damon, my brother, was with General Groom's army down in Atlanta, most of my boyhood friends were either about to be betrothed or on faraway battlefields themselves, and Father was constantly in his study.

'Gonna be a hot one!' our overseer, Robert, yelled from the edge of the barn, where he was watching two stable boys attempt to bridle one of the horses Father had purchased at auction last week.

'Yep,' I grunted. That was another problem: while I yearned for someone to talk with, when presented with a conversation partner, I was never content. What I desperately wanted was to meet someone who could understand me, who could discuss real things like books and life, not just the weather. Robert was nice enough and one of Father's most trusted advisers, but he was so loud and brash that even a ten-minute conversation could leave me exhausted.

'Heard the latest?' Robert asked, abandoning the horse to walk towards me. I groaned inwardly.

I shook my head. 'Haven't been reading the papers.

What's General Groom doing now?' I asked, even though conversation about the war always left me uneasy.

Robert shielded his eyes from the sun as he shook his head. 'No, not the war. The animal attacks. The folks over at Griffin's lost five chickens. All with gashes in their necks.'

I paused mid-step, the hairs on the back of my neck rising on end. All summer, reports of strange animal attacks had emerged from neighbouring plantations. Usually, the animals were small, mostly chickens or geese, but in the past few weeks someone – probably Robert, after four or five tumblers of whiskey – had begun a rumour that the attacks were the work of demons. I didn't believe that, but it was one more reminder that the world wasn't the same one I'd grown up in. Everything was changing, whether I wanted it to or not.

'Could have been a stray dog that killed them,' I told Robert with an impatient wave of my hand, parroting the words I'd overheard Father say to Robert last week. A breeze picked up, causing the horses to stomp their feet nervously.

'Well, then, I hope one of those stray dogs doesn't find you when you're out riding alone like you do every day.' With that, Robert strode off towards the pasture.

I walked into the cool, dark stable. The steady rhythm of the breathing and snorting of the horses relaxed me instantly. I plucked Mezzanotte's brush from the wall and began combing through her smooth, coal-black coat. She whinnied in appreciation.

Just then, the stable door creaked open, and Father stepped in. A tall man, Father carried himself with so much force and presence that he easily intimidated those who crossed his path. His face was lined with wrinkles that only added to his authority, and he wore a formal morning coat, despite the heat.

'Stefan?' Father called, glancing around the stalls. Even though he'd lived at Veritas for years, he'd probably only been in the stable a few times, preferring to have his horses prepared and brought straight to the door.

I ducked out of Mezzanotte's stall.

Father picked his way towards the back of the stable. His eyes flicked over me, and I felt suddenly embarrassed for him to see me caked in sweat and dirt. 'We have stable boys for a reason, son.'

'I know,' I said, feeling as though I'd disappointed him.

'There's a time and a place for having fun with horses. But then there's the point when it's time for a boy to stop playing and become a man.' Father hit Mezzanotte on the flanks, hard. She snorted and took a step back.

I clenched my jaw, waiting for him to tell me about how, when he was my age, he'd moved to Virginia from Italy with only the clothes on his back. How he'd fought and bargained to build a tiny, one-acre plot of land into what was now the two hundred acres of Veritas Estate. How he'd named it that because *veritas* was Latin for *truth*, because he'd learned that as long as a man searched for truth and fought deception, he didn't need anything else in life.

Father leaned against the door of the stall. 'Rosalyn Cartwright just celebrated her sixteenth birthday. She's looking for a husband.'

'Rosalyn Cartwright?' I repeated. When we were twelve, Rosalyn had gone to a finishing school outside of Richmond, and I hadn't seen her in ages. She was a nondescript girl with mousy blonde hair and brown eyes; in every memory I held of her, she wore a brown dress. She'd never been sunny and laughing, like Clementine Haverford, or flirty and feisty, like Amelia Hawke, or whip-smart and mischievous, like Sarah Brennan. She was simply a shadow in the background, content to trail along on all our childhood adventures but never to lead them.

'Yes. Rosalyn Cartwright.' Father gave me one of his rare smiles, with the corners of his lips turned so slightly upward, one would think he was sneering if one did not know him well. 'Her father and I have been talking, and it seems the ideal union. She's always been quite fond of you, Stefan.'

'I don't know if Rosalyn Cartwright and I are a match,' I mumbled, feeling as though the cool walls of the stable were closing in on me. Of *course* Father and Mr Cartwright had been talking. Mr Cartwright owned the bank in town; if Father had an alliance with him, it would be easy to expand Veritas even further. And if they'd been talking, it was as good as done that Rosalyn and I were to be man and wife.

'Of course you don't know, boy!' Father guffawed, slapping me on the back. He was in remarkably good spirits. My spirits, however, were sinking lower and lower with each word. I squeezed my eyes shut, hoping this was all a bad dream. 'No boy your age knows what's good for him. That's why you need to trust me. I'm arranging a dinner for next week to celebrate the two of you. In the meantime, pay her a call. Get to know her. Compliment her. Let her fall in love with you.' Father finished, taking my hand and pressing a box inside my palm.

What about me? What if I don't want her to fall in love with me? I wanted to say. But I didn't. Instead, I shoved the box in my back pocket without glancing at its contents, then went back to attending to Mezzanotte, brushing her so hard, she snorted and stepped back in indignation.

'I'm glad we had this talk, son,' Father said. I waited for him to notice that I'd barely said a word, to realize that it was absurd to ask me to marry a girl I hadn't spoken to in years.

'Father?' I said, hoping he would say something to set me free from the fate he'd laid out for me.

'I think October would be lovely for a wedding,' my father said instead, letting the door bang shut behind him.

I clenched my jaw in frustration. I thought back to

our childhood, when Rosalyn and I would find ourselves pushed to sit together at Saturday barbecues and church socials. But the forced socialization simply hadn't worked, and as soon as we were old enough to choose our own playmates, Rosalyn and I went our separate ways. Our relationship was going to be just as it was when we were ten years younger – ignoring each other while dutifully making our parents happy. Except now, I realized grimly, we'd be bound together forever.

CHAPTER
2

The next afternoon, I found myself sitting on a stiff, low-backed velvet chair in the Cartwrights' sitting room. Every time I shifted, trying to find a spot of comfort on the hard seat, I felt the gaze of Mrs Cartwright, Rosalyn and her maid fall upon me. It was as though I was the subject in a portrait at a museum or a character in a drawing room drama. The entire front room reminded me of a set for a play – it was hardly the type of place in which to relax. Or talk, for that matter. During the first fifteen minutes of my arrival, we'd haltingly discussed the weather, the new store in town and the war.

After that, long pauses reigned, the only sound the hollow clacking of the maid's knitting needles. I glanced at Rosalyn again, trying to find something about her person to compliment. She had a pert face with a dimple in her chin, and her earlobes were small and symmetrical. From the half inch of ankle I could see below the hem of her dress, it seemed she had delicate bone structure.

Just then a sharp pain shot up my leg. I let out a cry, then looked down at the floor, where a tiny, copper-coloured dog about the size of a rat had embedded its pointed teeth in the skin of my ankle.

'Oh, that's Penny. Penny's just saying hi, isn't she?' Rosalyn cooed, scooping up the tiny animal into her arms. The dog stared at me, continuing to bare its teeth. I inched farther back in my seat.

'She's, uh, very nice,' I said, even though I didn't understand the point of a dog that small. Dogs were supposed to be companions that could keep you company on a hunt, not ornaments to match the furniture.

'Isn't she, though?' Rosalyn looked up in rapture. 'She's my very best friend, and I must say, I'm terrified of her going outside now, with all the reports of animal murders!'

'I'm telling you, Stefan, we're so frightened!' Mrs Cartwright jumped in, running her hands over the bodice of her navy dress. 'I don't understand this world. It's simply not meant for us women to even go outside.'

'I hope whatever it is doesn't attack us. Sometimes I'm scared to step foot outdoors, even when it's light,' Rosalyn fretted, clutching Penny tightly to her chest. The dog yelped and jumped off her lap. 'I'd die if anything happened to Penny.'

'I'm sure she'll be fine. After all, the attacks have been happening on farms, not in town,' I said, halfheartedly trying to comfort her.

'Stefan?' Mrs Cartwright asked in her shrill voice, the same one she affected when she used to chide Damon and me for whispering during church. Her face was pinched, and her expression looked like she had just sucked on a lemon. 'Don't you think Rosalyn looks especially beautiful today?'

'Oh, yes,' I lied. Rosalyn was wearing a drab brown dress that matched her brownish blonde hair. Loose ringlets fell about her skinny shoulders. Her outfit was a direct contrast to the parlour, which was decorated with oak furniture, brocade chairs and dark-coloured Oriental rugs that overlapped on the gleaming wood floor. In the far corner, over the marble mantel, a portrait of Mr Cartwright stared down at me, a stern expression on his angular face. I glanced at him curiously. In contrast to his wife, who was overweight and red-faced, Mr Cartwright was ghostly pale and skinny – and slightly dangerous-looking, like the vultures we'd seen circling around the battlefield last summer. Considering who her parents were, Rosalyn had actually turned out remarkably well.

Rosalyn blushed. I shifted on the chair's edge, feeling the jewellery box in my rear pocket. I'd glanced at the ring last night, when sleep wouldn't come. I recognized it instantly. It was an emerald circled by diamonds, made by the finest craftsmen in Venice and worn by my mother until the day she died.

'So, Stefan? What do you think of pink?' Rosalyn asked, breaking me out of my reverie.

'I'm sorry, what?' I asked, distracted.

Mrs Cartwright shot me an irritated look.

'Pink? For the dinner next week? It's so kind of your father to plan it,' Rosalyn said, her face bright red as she stared at the floor.

'I think pink would look delightful on you. You'll be beautiful no matter what you wear,' I said woodenly, as though I were an actor reading lines from a script. Mrs Cartwright smiled approvingly. The dog ran to her and jumped onto a pillow next to her. She began stroking its coat.

Suddenly the room felt hot and humid. The cloying, competing scents of Mrs Cartwright's and Rosalyn's perfumes made my head spin. I sneaked a glance at the antique grandfather clock in the corner. I'd been here for only fifty-five minutes, yet it might as well have been fifty-five years.

I stood up, my legs wobbling beneath me. 'It has been lovely visiting with you, Mrs and Miss Cartwright, but I'd be loath to take up the rest of your afternoon.'

'Thank you.' Mrs Cartwright nodded, not rising from her settee. 'Maisy will show you out,' she said, lifting her chin towards their maid, who was now dozing over her knitting.

I breathed a sigh of relief as I left the house. The air was cool against my clammy skin, and I was happy that I hadn't had our coachman wait for me; I would be able to clear my head by walking the two miles home. The sun was beginning to sink into the horizon, and the smell of honeysuckle and jasmine hung heavily in the air.

I glanced up at Veritas as I strode up the hill. Blooming lilies surrounded the large urns flanking the path to the front door. The white columns of the porch glowed orange from the setting sun, the pond's mirror-like surface gleamed in the distance, and I could hear the faraway sound of the children playing near the servants' quarters. This was my home, and I loved it.

But I couldn't imagine sharing it with Rosalyn. I shoved my hands in my pockets and angrily kicked a stone in the curve of the road.

I paused when I reached the entrance to the drive, where an unfamiliar coach was standing. I stared with curiosity – we rarely had visitors – as a white-haired coachman jumped out of the driver's seat and opened the cab. A beautiful, pale woman with cascading dark curls stepped out. She wore a billowing white dress, cinched at her narrow waist with a peach-coloured ribbon. A matching peach hat was perched atop her head, obscuring her eyes.

As if she knew I was staring, she turned. I gasped despite myself. She was more than beautiful; she was sublime. Even from a distance of twenty paces, I could see her dark eyes flickering, her pink lips curving into a small smile. Her thin fingers touched the blue cameo necklace at her throat, and I found myself mirroring the gesture, imagining what her small hand would feel like on my own skin.

Then she turned again, and a woman, who must have been her maid, stepped out of the cab and began fussing with her skirts.

'Hello!' she called.

'Hello . . .' I croaked. As I breathed, I smelled a heady combination of ginger and lemon.

'I'm Katherine Pierce. And you are?' she asked, her voice playful. It was as if she knew I was tongue-tied by her beauty. I wasn't sure whether I should be mortified or thankful that she was taking the lead.

'Katherine,' I repeated slowly, remembering. Father had told me the story of a friend of a friend down in Atlanta. His neighbours had perished when their house caught fire during General Sherman's siege, and the only survivor had been a sixteen-year-old girl with no relations. Immediately, Father had offered to board the girl in our carriage house. It had all sounded very mysterious and romantic, and when Father told me, I saw in his eyes how much he enjoyed the idea of serving as rescuer to this young orphan.

'Yes,' she said, her eyes dancing. 'And you are . . .'

'Stefan!' I said quickly. 'Stefan Salvatore. Giuseppe's son. I am so sorry for your family's tragedy.'

'Thank you,' she said. In an instant, her eyes became dark and sombre. 'And I thank you and your father for hosting me and my maid, Emily. I don't know what we would have done without you.'

'Yes, of course.' I felt suddenly protective. 'You'll be in the carriage house. Would you like me to show you?'

'We shall find it ourselves. Thank you, Stefan Salvatore,' Katherine said, following the coachman, who carried a large trunk towards the small guest house, which was set back a bit from the main estate. Then she turned around and stared at me. 'Or should I call you Saviour Stefan?' she asked with a wink before turning on her heel.

I watched her walk into the sunset, her maid trailing her, and instantly I knew my life would never be the same.

CHAPTER

3

August 21, 1864
*I can't stop thinking about her. I will not even write
her name; I daren't. She is beautiful, entrancing,
singular. When I'm with Rosalyn, I am Giuseppe's
son, the Salvatore boy, essentially interchangeable
with Damon. I know it would not matter one whit to
the Cartwrights if Damon took my place. It is only me
because Father knew Damon would not stand for it,
knew I would say yes, just like always.*

*But when I saw her, her lithe figure, her red lips,
her eyes that were flickering and sad and thrilling all
at once . . . it was as though I was finally just myself,
just Stefan Salvatore.*

*I must be strong. I must treat her like a sister. I must
fall in love with the woman who is to be my wife.*

But I fear it is already too late . . .

Rosalyn Salvatore, I thought to myself the next day, tasting the words as I walked out the door, ready to fulfil my duty by paying a second call on my soon-to-be-betrothed. I imagined living with Rosalyn in the carriage house – or perhaps some smaller mansion my father would build as our wedding present – the working all day, pouring through ledgers with my father in his stuffy study, while she took care of our children. I tried to feel excitement. But all I felt was cold dread seeping through my veins.

I walked around the grand path of Veritas and gazed wistfully up at the carriage house. I hadn't seen Katherine since she'd arrived yesterday afternoon. Father had dispatched Alfred to invite her to supper, but she'd declined. I'd spent the evening looking out of the window towards the house, but I couldn't see any flicker of candlelight. If I hadn't known she and Emily had moved in, I'd have assumed the house had remained unoccupied. Finally, I went to sleep, wondering the whole time what Katherine was doing and whether she needed comforting.

I tore my eyes away from the drawn upstairs shades and trudged down the driveway. The dirt road under my feet was hard and cracked; we needed a good rainstorm. There was no breeze, and the air felt dead. There wasn't another person outside as far as the eye could see, yet as I walked, the hairs on the back of my neck stood on end, and I got the uneasy feeling that I wasn't alone. Unbidden, Robert's warnings about walking off on my own floated through my mind.

'Hello?' I called out as I turned around.

I started. Standing just a few feet behind me, leaning against one of the angel statues that flanked the drive, was Katherine. She wore a white sun bonnet that protected her ivory skin and a white dress dotted with tiny rosebuds. Despite the heat, her fair skin looked as cool as the pond on a December morning.

She smiled at me, displaying perfectly straight white teeth. 'I had hoped for a tour of the grounds, but it seems you are otherwise engaged.'

My heart pounded at the word 'engaged', the ring box in my back pocket as heavy as a branding iron. 'I'm not . . . no. I mean,' I stammered, 'I could stay.'

'Nonsense.' Katherine shook her head. 'I already am taking lodging from you and your father. I will not take your time as well.' She raised a dark eyebrow at me.

Never before had I spoken with a girl who seemed so at ease and sure of herself. I felt the sudden, overwhelming urge to whip the ring from my pocket and offer it to Katherine on one knee. But then I thought of Father and forced my hand to stay put.

'May I at least walk with you for a bit?' Katherine asked, swinging her sun umbrella back and forth.

Companionably, we walked down the road. I kept glancing to my left and right, wondering why she didn't seem nervous to walk, unaccompanied, with a man. Perhaps it was because she was an orphan and so utterly alone in the world. Whatever the reason, I was grateful for it.

A light wind blew around us, and I inhaled her lemony ginger scent, feeling as though I could die of happiness, right there, next to Katherine. Simply being near her was a reminder that beauty and love did exist in the world, even if I couldn't have them.

'I think I shall call you Silent Stefan,' Katherine said as we walked through the cluster of oaks that marked the line between the village of Mystic Falls and the outlying plantations and estates.

'I'm sorry . . .' I started, fearing that I was as dull to her as Rosalyn was to me. 'It's simply that we don't get very many strangers in Mystic Falls. It's difficult to speak to someone who doesn't know my whole history. I suppose I don't want to bore you. After Atlanta, I'm sure you find Mystic Falls a bit quiet.' I felt mortified as soon as the sentence left my lips. Her parents had *died* in Atlanta, and here I was, making it sound like she'd left some exciting life to live here. I cleared my throat. 'I mean, not that you had found Atlanta exciting, or that you wouldn't enjoy getting away from everything.'

Katherine smiled. 'Thank you, Stefan. That's sweet.' Her tone made it clear she didn't want to delve into the topic any further.

We walked in silence for a few long moments. I kept my stride deliberately short so Katherine could keep up. Then, whether by accident or by design I'm not sure, Katherine's fingers brushed against my arm. They were cold as ice, even in the humid air. 'Just so you know,' she said, 'I don't find *anything* about you boring.'

My entire body flamed hot as a conflagration. I glanced up the road, as if trying to ascertain the best route for us to follow, though really I was hiding my blush from Katherine. I felt the weight of the ring in my pocket again, heavier than ever.

I turned to face her, to say what, I'm not even sure. But she was no longer by my side.

'Katherine?' I called, shielding my eyes against the sun, waiting for her lilting laugh to rise up in the underbrush along the road. But all I heard was the echo of my own voice. She had vanished.

CHAPTER

4

I didn't call on the Cartwrights that day. Instead, after searching the path, I sprinted the two miles back to the estate, terrified that Katherine had somehow been dragged into the forest by some unseen hand – perhaps by the very creature that had been terrorizing the nearby plantations.

When I arrived home, though, I found her on the porch swing, chatting with her maid, a sweating glass of lemonade beside her. Her skin was pale, her eyes languorous, as if she'd never run a day in her life. How had she gotten back to the carriage house so quickly? I wanted to stride up and ask, but I stopped myself. I'd sound like a madman, recounting the whirling thoughts in my head.

At that moment, Katherine glanced up and shielded her eyes. 'Back so soon?' she called, as if surprised to see me. I nodded dumbly as she slid off the porch swing and glided into the carriage house.

The image of her smiling face kept floating back to me the next day, when I forced myself to make the call on Rosalyn. It was even worse than the first call. Mrs Cartwright sat right beside me on the couch, and every time I shifted, her eyes gleamed, as if she was expecting me to take out the ring at any second. I'd choked out some questions about Penny, about the puppies she'd had last June, and about the progress Honoria Fells, the town dressmaker, had made on Rosalyn's pink gown. But no matter how much I tried, all I wanted was an excuse to leave so I could visit with Katherine.

Finally, I muttered something about not wanting to be out past dark. According to Robert, there had been three more animal killings, including George Brower's horse right outside the apothecary. I almost felt guilty as Mrs Cartwright ushered me out of the house and into my carriage, as if I were going off to battle rather than a two-mile ride home.

When I got to the estate, my heart fell when I saw no sign of Katherine. I was about to double back to the stable to brush Mezzanotte when I heard angry voices emanating from the open windows of the kitchen of the main house.

'No son of mine will *ever* disobey me! You need to go back and take your place in the world.' It was Father's voice, tinged with the heavy Italian accent that became apparent only when he was extremely upset.

'My *place* is here. The army is not for me. What is so wrong about following my own mind?' another voice yelled, confident, proud and angry all at once.

Damon.

My heart quickened as I stepped into the kitchen and saw my brother. Damon was my closest friend, the person I looked up to most in the world – even more than Father, though I'd never admitted it out loud. I hadn't seen him since last year, when he joined General Groom's army. He looked taller, his hair somehow seemed darker, and the skin on his neck was sun-darkened and freckled.

I threw my arms around him, thankful I had arrived home when I did. He and Father had never gotten along, and their fights occasionally escalated to blows.

'Brother!' He slapped my back as he pulled out of the embrace.

'We're not finished, Damon,' my father warned as he retreated to his study.

Damon turned to me. 'I see Father's the same as always.'

'He's not so bad.' I always felt awkward speaking badly of Father, even as I chafed against my forced engagement to Rosalyn. 'Did you just get back?' I asked, changing the subject. Damon smiled. There were slight lines around his eyes that no one would notice unless they knew him well.

'An hour ago. I couldn't miss my younger brother's engagement announcement, could I?' he asked, a slight hint of sarcasm in his voice. 'Father told me all about it. Seems that he's depending on you to carry on the Salvatore name. And just think, by the time of the Founders Ball, you'll be a husband!'

I stiffened. I'd forgotten about the ball. It was the event of the year, and Father, Sheriff Forbes and Mayor Lockwood had been planning it for months. Partly a war benefit, partly an opportunity for the town to enjoy the last gasp of summer and mostly a chance for the town leaders to pat themselves on the backs, the Founders Ball had always been one of my favourite Mystic Falls traditions. Now I dreaded it.

Damon must have sensed my discomfort, because he started digging through his canvas rucksack. It was filthy and had what looked like a bloodstain on the corner. Finally, he pulled out a large, misshapen leather ball, much larger and more oblong than a baseball. 'Want to play?' he asked, palming the ball from hand to hand.

'What is that?' I asked.

'A football. Me and the boys play when we've got time away from the field. It'll be good for you. Get some colour in your cheeks. We don't want you getting soft,' he said, imitating my father's voice so perfectly that I had to laugh.

Damon walked out the door, and I followed, shrugging off my linen jacket. Suddenly the sunshine felt warmer, the grass felt softer, everything felt *better* than it had just minutes before.

'Catch!' Damon yelled, finding me off guard. I lifted up my arms and caught the ball against my chest.

'Can I play?' a female voice asked, breaking the moment.

Katherine. She was wearing a simple, lilac summer shift dress, and her hair was pulled into a bun at the base of her neck. I noticed that her dark eyes perfectly complemented the brilliant blue cameo necklace that rested in the hollow of her throat. I imagined lacing my fingers through her delicate hands, then kissing her white neck.

I forced myself to tear my gaze away from her. 'Katherine, this is my brother, Damon. Damon, this is Katherine Pierce. She is staying with us,' I said stiffly, glancing back and forth between them to gauge his reaction. Katherine's eyes danced, as if she found my formality incredibly amusing. So did Damon's.

'Damon, I can tell you're just as sweet as your brother,' she said in an exaggerated Southern accent. Even though it was a phrase any of the girls in the county would use when talking to a man, it sounded vaguely mocking coming from her lips.

'We'll see about that.' Damon smiled. 'So, brother, shall we let Katherine play?'

'I don't know,' I said, suddenly hesitant. 'What are the rules?'

'Who needs rules?' Katherine asked, flashing a grin that revealed her perfectly straight white teeth.

I turned the ball in my hand. 'My brother plays rough,' I warned.

'Somehow I think I play rougher.' In one swoop, Katherine grabbed the ball from my grasp. As they had been the previous day, her hands were cold, like ice, despite the heat of the afternoon. Her touch sent a jolt of energy through my body and up to my brain. 'Loser has to groom my horses!' she called as the wind whipped her hair behind her.

Damon watched her run, then arched an eyebrow towards me. 'That is a girl who wants to be chased.' With that, Damon dug his heels into the earth and ran, his powerful body hurtling down the hill towards the pond.

After a second, I ran, too. I felt the wind whip around my ears. 'I'll get you!' I yelled. It was a phrase I'd have yelled when I was eight and playing games with the girls my age, but I felt that the stakes of this game were higher than anything I'd ever played in my life.

CHAPTER
5

The next morning, I awoke to breathless news from Rosalyn's servants that her prized dog, Penny, had been attacked. Mrs Cartwright summoned me to her daughter's chambers, saying nothing had stopped Rosalyn from crying. I tried to comfort her, but her wracking sobs never abated.

The whole time, Mrs Cartwright kept giving me disapproving glances, as if I should be doing a better job calming Rosalyn.

'You have me,' I'd said at one point, if only to appease her. At that, Rosalyn had flung her arms around me, crying so hard into my shoulder that her tears left a wet mark on my waistcoat. I tried to be sympathetic, but I felt a stab of annoyance at the way she was carrying on. After all, I'd never carried on like that when my mother had died. Father hadn't let me.

You have to be strong, a fighter, he'd said at the funeral. And so I was. I didn't cry when, just a week after Mother's death, our nanny, Cordelia, began absentmindedly humming the French lullaby Mother had always sung. Not when Father took down the portrait of Mother that had hung in the front room. Not even when Artemis, Mother's favourite horse, had to be put down.

'Did you see the dog?' Damon asked, as we walked into town together that night to get a drink at the tavern. Now that the dinner where I was to publicly propose to Rosalyn was just days away, we were heading out for a whiskey to celebrate my impending nuptials. At least, that's what Damon called it, elongating his accent to a flat Charlestonian drawl and wiggling his eyebrows as he said it. I tried to smile as if I thought it was a great joke, but if I began talking, I knew I wouldn't be able to hold back my dismay about marrying Rosalyn. And there wasn't anything wrong with her. It was just . . . it was just that she wasn't Katherine.

I turned my thoughts back to Penny. 'Yes. Its throat had a gash in it, but whatever the animal was didn't go for her innards. Strange, right?' I said as I rushed to keep up with him. The army had made him stronger and faster. 'It's a strange time, brother,' Damon said. 'Maybe it's the Yankees,' he teased with a smirk.

As we walked down the cobblestone streets, I noticed signs affixed to most doorways. A reward of one hundred dollars was being offered to anyone who found the wild animal responsible for the attacks. I stared at the sign. Maybe *I* could find it, then take the money and buy a train ticket to Boston, or New York, or some city where no one could find me and no one had ever heard of Rosalyn Cartwright. I smiled to myself; that would be something Damon might actually do – he never worried about consequences or other people's feelings. I was about to point out the sign and ask what he'd do with one hundred dollars when I saw someone frantically waving at us in front of the apothecary.

'Are those the Salvatore brothers?' a voice called from up the street. I squinted across the twilight and saw Pearl, the apothecary, standing outside her shop with her daughter, Anna. Pearl and Anna were two more victims of the war. Pearl's husband had died at the Vicksburg siege just last spring. After that, Pearl had found a home in Mystic Falls, and she ran an apothecary that was always busy. Jonathan Gilbert, in particular, was almost always there when I walked by, complaining about some ailment or purchasing some remedy or another. Town gossip was that he fancied her.

'Pearl, you remember my brother, Damon?' I called as we walked over the square to greet them.

Pearl smiled and nodded. Her face was unlined, and a game among the girls was trying to determine how old she was. She had a daughter who was only a few years younger than me, so she couldn't be that young. 'You two certainly look handsome,' she said fondly. Anna was the spitting image of her mother, and when they stood side by side, the two looked as if they could be sisters.

'Anna, you look more beautiful each year. Are you old enough to be going to dances yet?' Damon asked, a twinkle in his eyes. I smiled despite myself. Of course Damon would be able to charm both a mother and a daughter.

'Almost,' Anna said, her eyes sparkling in anticipation. Fifteen was the age when girls were old enough to stay through dinner and hear the band strike up a waltz.

Pearl used a wrought-iron key to lock the apothecary, then turned to face us. 'Damon, can you do me a favour? Can you make sure Katherine gets on tomorrow night? She's a lovely girl, and, well, you know how people talk about strangers. I knew her in Atlanta.'

'I promise,' Damon said solemnly.

I stiffened. Was Damon escorting Katherine tomorrow night? I hadn't thought she'd come to the party, and I couldn't imagine proposing in front of her. But what choice did I have? Tell Father that Katherine wasn't invited? Not propose to Rosalyn?

'Have fun tonight, boys,' Pearl said, breaking me out of my reverie.

'Wait!' I called, the dinner momentarily forgotten.

Pearl turned round, a quizzical expression on her face.

'It's dark, and there have been more attacks. Would you like us to escort you ladies home?' I asked.

Pearl shook her head. 'Anna and I are strong women. We'll be fine. Besides . . .' She blushed and glanced around, as if afraid to be overheard. 'I believe Jonathan Gilbert wants to do that for us. But I do thank you for your concern.'

Damon wiggled his eyebrows and let out a low whistle. 'You know how I feel about strong women,' he whispered.

'Damon. Be appropriate,' I said, slugging him on the shoulder. After all, he wasn't on the battlefields any more. He was in Mystic Falls, a town where people liked to eavesdrop and loved to talk. Had he forgotten so quickly?

'Okay, Auntie Stefan!' Damon teased, raising his voice in a high lisp. I laughed despite myself and slugged him again on the arm for good measure. The punch was light, but felt good – a way to unleash some of my annoyance that he was able to escort Katherine to the dinner.

He good-naturedly slugged me back, and we would have broken out into an all-out brotherly brawl if Damon hadn't pushed open the wooden door to the Mystic Falls Tavern. We were immediately greeted by an enthusiastic smile from the voluptuous, red-haired barmaid behind the counter. It was clear that Damon had made himself at home here on several occasions.

We elbowed our way to the back of the tavern.

The room smelled of sawdust and sweat, and men in uniform were everywhere. Some had bandages on their heads, others wore slings and some hobbled to the counter on crutches. I recognized Henry, a dark-skinned soldier who practically lived at the tavern, drinking whiskey alone in a corner. Robert had told me stories about him: he never socialized with anyone, and no one ever saw him in the light of day. There was talk that maybe he was associated with the attacks, but how could he be, if he was always at the tavern?

I peeled my eyes away to take in the rest of the scene. There were older men tightly grouped in a corner, playing cards and drinking whiskey and, in the opposite corner, a few women. I could tell from the rouge on their cheeks and their painted fingernails that they weren't the types to spend time with our childhood playmates, Clementine Haverford or Amelia Hawke. As we walked past, one of them brushed my arm with her painted fingernails.

'You like it here?' Damon pulled out a wooden table from the wall, an amused smile on his face.

'I suppose I do.' I plunked down on the hard wooden bench and surveyed my surroundings once again. Being in the tavern, I felt I'd stumbled into a secret society of men, just one more thing I knew I'd have little chance to discover before I was a married man and expected to be at home every evening.

'I'll get us some drinks,' Damon said, making his way to the bar. I watched as he rested his elbows on the counter and talked easily to the barmaid, who tilted her head back and laughed as if he'd said something hilarious. Which he probably had. That's why all women fell in love with him.

'So, how does it feel to be a married man?'

I turned round to see Dr Janes behind me. Well into his seventies, Dr Janes was slightly senile and often loudly proclaimed to anyone who'd listen that his longevity was due exclusively to his prodigious indulgence in whiskey.

'Not married yet, Doctor.' I smiled tightly, wishing Damon would come back with our drinks.

'Ah, my boy, but you will be. Mr Cartwright at the bank has been discussing it for weeks. The fair young Rosalyn. Quite a catch!' Dr Janes continued loudly. I glanced around, hoping no one had heard.

At that moment, Damon appeared and gently set our whiskeys on the table. 'Thank you,' I said, drinking mine down in one gulp. Dr Janes hobbled away.

'That thirsty, huh?' Damon asked, taking a small sip of his own drink.

I shrugged. In the past, I'd never kept secrets from my brother. But talking about Rosalyn felt dangerous. Somehow, no matter what I said or felt, I still had to marry her. If anyone heard even an inkling of regret from me, there'd be no end to the talk.

Suddenly, a new whiskey appeared in front of me. I glanced up to see the pretty bartender Damon had been talking to standing over our table.

'You look like you need this. Seems you've had a rough day.' The barmaid winked one of her green eyes and set the sweating tumbler on the rough-hewn wooden table in front of me.

'Thank you,' I said as I took a small, grateful sip.

'Any time,' the barmaid said, her crinoline skirts swishing over her hips. I watched her retreating back. All the women in the tavern, even those with loose reputations, were more interesting than Rosalyn. But no matter who I glanced at, the only image that filled my mind was Katherine's face.

'Alice likes you,' Damon observed.

I shook my head. 'You know I can't look. By the end of summer, I'll be a married man. You, meanwhile, are free to do as you please.' I'd meant it to be an observation, but the words came out as a judgment.

'That's true,' Damon said. 'But you do know you don't *have* to do something just because Father says so, right?'

'It's not that simple.' I clenched my jaw. Damon couldn't understand because he was wild and untamable – so much so that Father had entrusted me, the younger brother, with the future of Veritas, a role I now found stifling.

A sliver of betrayal shot through me at this thought – that it was Damon's fault I had to shoulder so much responsibility. I shook my head, as if trying to remove the idea from it, and took another drink of whiskey.

'It's very simple,' Damon said, oblivious to my momentary annoyance. 'Just tell him you are not in love with Rosalyn. That you need to find your own place in the world and can't just follow someone's orders blindly. That's what I learned in the army: you have to believe in what you do. Otherwise, what's the point?'

I shook my head. 'I'm not like you. I trust Father. And I know he only wants the best. It's just that I wish . . . I wish I had more time,' I said finally. It was true. Maybe I could grow to love Rosalyn, but the thought that I could be married and have a child in just one short year filled me with dread. 'But it'll be fine,' I said with finality. It *had* to be.

'What do you think of our new houseguest?' I said, changing the subject.

Damon smiled. 'Katherine,' he said, drawing the name into the full three syllables, as if he could taste it on his tongue. 'Now, she's a girl who's difficult to figure out, don't you agree?'

'I suppose,' I said, glad that Damon didn't know that I was dreaming of Katherine at night, and by day pausing at the door to the carriage house to see if I could hear her laughing with her maid; once I even stopped by the stable to smell the broad back of her horse, Clover, just to see if her lemon and ginger scent had lingered. It hadn't, and at that moment, in the barn surrounded by the horses, I'd realized how unbalanced I was becoming.

'They don't make girls like her in Mystic Falls.

Do you think she has a soldier somewhere?' Damon asked.

'No!' I said, annoyed once again. 'She's in *mourning* for her *parents*. I hardly think she's looking for a beau.'

'Of course.' Damon knit his eyebrows together contritely. 'And I wasn't presuming anything. But if she needs a shoulder to cry on, I'd be happy to lend it to her.'

I shrugged. Even though I'd brought up the subject, I was no longer sure I wanted to hear what Damon thought of her. In fact, as beautiful as she was, I almost wished that some far-flung relatives from Charleston or Richmond or Atlanta would step forward to invite her to live with them. If she were out of sight, then maybe I could somehow force myself to love Rosalyn.

Damon stared at me, and I knew in that moment how miserable I must have looked. 'Cheer up, brother,' he said. 'The night is young, and the whiskey's on me.'

But there wasn't enough whiskey in all of Virginia to make me love Rosalyn . . . or forget about Katherine.

CHAPTER
6

The weather didn't break by my engagement dinner a few days later, and even at five o'clock in the afternoon the air was hot and humid. In the kitchen, I'd overheard the servants gossiping that the strange, still weather was a result of the animal-killing demons. But discussion of the demons did not stop people from all over the county coming to the Grange Hall to celebrate the Confederacy. The coaches backed up beyond the stone drive and showed no sign of slowing their onslaught towards the imposing stone structure.

'Stefan Salvatore!' I heard as I stepped out of the coach behind my father.

As my feet hit dirt, I saw Ellen Emerson and her daughter, Daisy, walking arm in arm, trailed by two maids. Hundreds of lanterns lit the stone steps leading to the white wooden doors, and carriages lined the curved walkway. I could hear strains of a waltz coming from inside the hall.

'Mrs Emerson. Daisy.' I bowed deeply. Daisy had hated me ever since we were children, when Damon had dared me to push her into Willow Creek.

'Why, if it isn't the handsome Emerson ladies,' Father said, also bowing. 'Thank you to both of you for coming to this small supper. It's so good to see everyone in town. We need to band together, now more than ever,' Father said, catching Ellen Emerson's eye.

'Stefan,' Daisy repeated, nodding as she took my hand.

'Daisy. You look more beautiful every day. Can you please forgive a gentleman for his wicked youth?'

She glared at me. I sighed. There was no mystery or intrigue in Mystic Falls. Everyone knew everyone else. If Rosalyn and I were to get married, our children would be dancing with Daisy's children. They would have the same conversations, the same jokes, the same fights. And the cycle would continue for eternity.

'Ellen, would you do me the honour of allowing me to show you inside?' Father asked, anxious to make sure the hall was decorated according to his exacting specifications. Daisy's mother nodded, and Daisy and I were left under the watchful gaze of the Emersons' maid.

'I've heard Damon's back. How is he?' Daisy asked,

finally deigning to talk to me.

'Miss Emerson, we best be going inside to find your mama,' Daisy's maid interrupted, tugging Daisy's arm through the wide double doors of the Grange Hall.

'I look forward to seeing Damon. Do give him that message!' Daisy called over her shoulder.

I sighed and stepped into the hall. Located between town and the estate, the Grange had once been a meeting spot for the county's landed gentry but had now become a makeshift armoury. The walls of the hall were covered with ivy and wisteria and, farther up, Confederate flags. A band on the raised stage in the corner played a jaunty rendition of 'The Bonnie Blue Flag', and at least fifty couples circled the floor with glasses of punch in their hands. Father had obviously spared no expense, and it was clear that this was more than a simple welcome dinner for the troops.

Heart-heavy, I headed over to the punch.

I hadn't walked more than five steps when I felt a hand clap my back. I prepared myself to give a tight smile and accept the awkward congratulations that were already trickling in. What was the point of having a dinner to announce an engagement that everyone seemed to know about, I thought sourly.

I turned to find myself face-to-face with Mr Cartwright. I instantly composed my expression into something I hoped resembled excitement.

'Stefan, boy! If it isn't the man of the hour!' Mr

Cartwright said, offering me a glass of whiskey.

'Sir. Thank you for allowing me the pleasure of your daughter's company,' I said automatically, taking the smallest sip I could muster. I'd woken up with a terrible whiskey headache the morning after Damon and I spent time at the tavern. I'd stayed in bed, a cool compress on my forehead, while Damon had barely seemed affected. I'd heard him chasing Katherine through the labyrinth in the backyard. Every laugh I'd heard was like a tiny dagger in my brain.

'The pleasure is all yours. I know it's a good merger. Practical and low risk with plenty of opportunity for growth.'

'Thank you, sir,' I said. 'And I am so sorry about Rosalyn's dog.'

Mr Cartwright shook his head. 'Don't tell my wife or Rosalyn, but I'd always hated the damn thing. Not saying it should have gone and gotten itself killed, but I think everyone is getting themselves all worked up over nothing. All this discussion of demons you hear all over the damn place. People whispering that the town is cursed. It's that kind of talk that makes people so afraid of risk. Makes them nervous about putting their money in the bank,' Mr Cartwright boomed, causing several people to stare. I smiled nervously.

Out of the corner of my eye I saw Father acting as host and shuttling people towards the long table at the centre of the room. I noticed each place was set with Mother's delicate fleur-de-lis china.

'Stefan,' my father said, clapping his hand on my shoulder, 'are you ready? You have everything you need?'

'Yes.' I touched the ring in my breast pocket and followed him to the head of the table. Rosalyn stood next to her mother and smiled tightly at her parents. Rosalyn's eyes, still red from crying over poor Penny, clashed horribly with the oversize, frilly pink dress she was wearing.

As our neighbours took their seats around us, I realized that there were still two empty seats to my left.

'Where's your brother?' Father asked, lowering his voice.

I glanced towards the door. The band was still playing, and there was anticipation in the air. Finally, the doors opened with a clatter, and Damon and Katherine walked in. Together.

It wasn't fair, I thought savagely. Damon could act like a boy, could continue to drink and flirt as if nothing had consequence. I'd always done the right thing, the responsible thing, and now it felt as though I was being punished for it by being forced to become a man.

Even I was surprised by the surge of anger I felt. Instantly guilty, I tried to squelch the emotion by downing the full glass of wine to my left. After all, would Katherine have been expected to come to the dinner by herself? And wasn't Damon just being gallant, the good elder brother?

Besides, they had no future. Marriages, at least in our society, were approved only if they merged two families. And, as an orphan, what did Katherine have to offer besides beauty? Father would never let me marry her, but that also meant he wouldn't let Damon marry her either. And even Damon wouldn't go so far as to marry someone Father didn't approve of. Right?

Still, I couldn't tear my eyes away from Damon's arm around Katherine's tiny waist. She wore a green muslin dress whose fabric spread across her hoop skirts, and there was a hushed murmur as she and Damon made their way to the two empty seats at the centre of the table. Her blue necklace gleamed at her throat, and she winked at me before taking the empty seat next to my own. Her hip brushed against mine, and I shifted uncomfortably.

'Damon.' Father nodded tersely as Damon sat down to his left.

'So do you think the army will be all the way down to Georgia by winter?' I asked Jonah Palmer loudly, simply because I didn't trust myself to speak to Katherine. If I heard her musical voice, I might lose my nerve to propose to Rosalyn.

'I'm not worried about Georgia. What I am worried about is getting the militia together to solve the problems here in Mystic Falls. These attacks will not be stood for,' Jonah, the town veterinarian who had also been training the Mystic Falls militia, said loudly, pounding his fist on the table so hard the china rattled.

Just then, an army of servants entered the hall, holding plates of wild pheasant. I took my silver fork and pushed the gamey meat around my plate; I had no appetite. Around me, I could hear the usual discussions: about the war, about what we could do for our boys in grey, about upcoming dinners and barbecues and church socials. Katherine was nodding intently at Honoria Fells across the table. Suddenly I felt jealous of the grizzled, frizzy-haired Honoria. She was able to have the one-on-one conversation with Katherine that I so desperately wanted.

'Ready, son?' Father elbowed me in the ribs, and I noticed that people were already finished with their meals. More wine was being poured, and the band, who'd paused during the main course, was playing in the corner. This was the moment everyone had been waiting for: they knew an announcement was about to be made, and they knew that following that announcement there would be celebrating and dancing. It was always the way dinners happened in Mystic Falls. But I'd never before been at the centre of an announcement. As if on cue, Honoria leaned towards me, and Damon smiled encouragingly.

Feeling sick to my stomach, I took a deep breath and clinked my knife against my crystal glass. Immediately, there was a hush throughout the hall, and even the servants stopped mid-step to stare at me.

I stood up, took a long swig of red wine for courage, and cleared my throat.

'I . . . um,' I began in a low, strained voice I didn't recognize as my own. 'I have an announcement.' Out of the corner of my eye, I saw Father clutching his champagne flute, ready to jump in with a toast. I glanced at Katherine. She was looking at me, her dark eyes piercing my own. I tore my gaze away and gripped my glass so tightly, I was sure it would break. 'Rosalyn, I'd like to ask for your hand in marriage. Will you do me the honour?' I said in a rush, fumbling in my suit pocket for the ring.

I pulled out the box and knelt down in front of Rosalyn, staring up at her watery brown eyes. 'For you,' I said without inflection, flipping open the lid and holding it out towards her.

Rosalyn shrieked, and the room burst into a smattering of applause. I felt a hand clap my back, and I saw Damon grinning down at me. Katherine clapped politely, an unreadable expression on her face.

'Here.' I took Rosalyn's tiny white hand and pushed the ring on her finger. It was too large, and the emerald rolled lopsidedly towards her pinkie. She looked like a child playing dress-up with her mother's jewellery. But Rosalyn didn't seem to care that the ring didn't fit. Instead, she held out her hand, watching as the diamonds captured the light of the table's candles. Immediately, a crush of women surrounded us, cooing over the ring.

'This does call for a celebration!' my father called out. 'Cigars for everyone. Come here, Stefan, son! You've made me one proud father.'

I nodded and shakily stepped over to him. It was ironic that while I'd spent my entire life trying to get my father's approval, what made him happiest was an act that made me feel dead inside.

'Katherine, will you dance with me?' I heard Damon's voice above the din of scraping chairs and clinking glassware. I stopped in my tracks, waiting for the answer.

Katherine glanced up, casting a furtive look in my direction. Her eyes held my own for a long moment. A wild urge to rip the ring off Rosalyn's finger and place it on Katherine's pale one nearly overtook me. But then Father nudged me from behind, and before I could react, Damon grabbed Katherine by the hand and led her out to the dance floor.

CHAPTER
7

The next week passed in a blur. I ran from fittings at Mrs Fells's dress shop to visits with Rosalyn in the Cartwrights' stuffy parlour to the tavern with Damon. I tried to forget Katherine, leaving my shutters closed so I wouldn't be tempted to look across the lawn at the carriage house, and forcing myself to smile and wave at Damon and Katherine when they explored the gardens.

Once I went up to the attic to look at the portrait of Mother. I wondered what advice she'd have for me. *Love is patient*, I remembered her saying in her lilting French accent during Bible study. The notion comforted me. Maybe love *could* come to me and Rosalyn.

After that, I tried to love Rosalyn, or at least garner some kind of affection for her. I knew, behind her quietness and her dishwater blonde hair, she was simply a sweet girl who'd make a doting wife and mother. Our most recent visits hadn't been awful. In fact, Rosalyn had been in remarkably good spirits. She'd gotten a new dog, a sleek black beast named Sadie, which she'd taken to carrying everywhere lest the new puppy suffer the same fate as Penny had. At one point, when Rosalyn looked up at me with adoring eyes, asking if I'd prefer lilacs or gardenias at the wedding, I almost felt fond of her. Maybe that would be enough.

Father had wasted no time in planning another party to celebrate. This time, it was a barbecue at the estate, and Father had invited everyone within a twenty-mile radius. I recognized only a handful of the young men, pretty girls and Confederate soldiers who milled around the labyrinth, acting as if they owned the estate. When I was younger, I used to love the parties at Veritas – they were always a chance to run down to the ice pond with our friends, to play hide-and-seek in the swamp, to ride horses to the Wickery Bridge, then dare each other to dive into the icy depths of Willow Creek. Now I just wished it were over, so I could be alone in my room.

'Stefan, care to share a whiskey with me?' Robert called out to me from the makeshift bar set up on the portico. To judge from his lopsided grin, he was already drunk.

He passed me a sweating tumbler and tipped his own to mine. 'Pretty soon, there will be young

Salvatores all over the place. Can you picture it?' He swept his hands expansively over the grounds as if to show me just how much room my imaginary family would have in which to grow.

I swirled my whiskey miserably, unable to picture it for myself.

'Well, you've made your daddy one lucky man. And Rosalyn one lucky girl,' Robert said. He lifted his glass to me one last time, then went to chat with the Lockwoods' overseer.

I sighed and sat down on the porch swing, observing the merriment occurring all around me. I knew I should feel happy. I knew Father only wanted what was best for me. I knew that there was nothing *wrong* with Rosalyn.

So why did this engagement feel like a death sentence?

On the lawn, people were eating and laughing and dancing, and a makeshift band made up of my childhood friends Ethan Giffin, Brian Walsh and Matthew Hartnett was playing a version of 'The Bonnie Blue Flag'. The sky was cloudless and the weather balmy, with just a slight nip in the air to remind us that it was, indeed, autumn. In the distance, schoolchildren were swinging and shrieking on the gate. To be around so much merriment – all meant for me – and not feel happy made my heart thud heavily in my chest.

Standing up, I walked inside towards Father's study. I shut the door to the study and breathed a sigh of relief. Only the faintest stream of sunlight peeked through the heavy damask curtains. The room was cool and smelled of well-oiled leather and musty books. I took out a slim volume of Shakespeare's sonnets and turned to my favourite poem. Shakespeare calmed me, the words soothing my brain and reminding me that there was love and beauty in the world. Perhaps experiencing it through art would be enough to sustain me.

I settled into Father's leather club chair in the corner and absentmindedly skimmed the onion-skin pages. I'm not sure how long I sat there, letting the language wash over me, but the more I read, the calmer I felt.

'What are you reading?'

The voice startled me, and the book slid off my lap with a clatter.

Katherine stood at the study entrance, wearing a simple white silk dress that hugged every curve of her body. All the other women at the party were wearing layers of crinoline and muslin, their skin guarded under thick fabric. But Katherine didn't seem the least bit embarrassed by her exposed white shoulders. Out of propriety, I glanced away.

'Why aren't you at the party?' I asked, bending to pick up my book.

Katherine stepped towards me. 'Why aren't *you* at the party? Aren't you the guest of honour?' She perched on the arm of my chair.

'Have you read Shakespeare?' I asked, gesturing to

the open book on my lap. It was a lame attempt to change the conversation; I had yet to meet a girl versed in his works. Just yesterday, Rosalyn had admitted she hadn't even read a book in the past three years, ever since she had graduated from the Girls Academy. Even at that, the last volume she'd perused was merely a primer on how to be a dutiful Confederate wife.

'Shakespeare,' she repeated, her accent expanding the word to three syllables. It was an odd accent, not one that I'd heard from other people from Atlanta. She swung her legs back and forth, and I could see that she wasn't wearing stockings. I tore my eyes away.

'*Shall I compare thee to a summer's day?*' she quoted.

I looked up, astonished. '*Thou art more lovely and more temperate,*' I said, continuing the quote. My heart galloped in my chest, and my brain felt as slow as molasses, creating an unusual sensation that made me feel I was dreaming.

Katherine yanked the book off my lap, closing it with a resounding clap. 'No,' she said firmly.

'But that's how the next line goes,' I said, annoyed that she was changing the rules of a game I thought I understood.

'That's how the next line goes for Mr Shakespeare. But I was simply asking you a question. Shall I compare you to a summer's day? Are you worthy of that comparison, Mr Salvatore? Or do you need a book to decide?' Katherine asked, grinning as she held the volume just out of my reach.

I cleared my throat, my mind racing. Damon would have said something witty in response, without even thinking about it. But when I was with Katherine, I was like a schoolboy who tries to impress a girl with a frog caught from the pond.

'Well, you could compare my brother to a summer's day. You've been spending a lot of time with him.' My face reddened, and instantly I wished I could take it back. I sounded so jealous and petty.

'Maybe a summer's day with a few thunderstorms in the distance,' Katherine said, arching her eyebrow. 'But you, Scholarly Stefan, you are different from Dark Damon. Or . . .' – she looked away, a flicker of a grin crossing her face – 'Dashing Damon.'

'I can be dashing, too,' I said petulantly, before I even realized what I was saying. I shook my head, frustrated. It was as though Katherine somehow compelled me to speak without thinking. She was so lively and vivacious – talking to her, I felt as though I was in a dream, where nothing I said would have any consequence but everything I said was important.

'Well, then, I must see that, Stefan,' Katherine said. She placed her icy hand on my forearm. 'I've gotten to know Damon, but I barely know you. It's quite a shame, don't you think?'

In the distance, the band struck up 'I'm a Good Old Rebel.' I knew I needed to get back outside, to smoke a cigar with Mr Cartwright, to twirl Rosalyn in a first waltz, to toast my place as a man of Mystic

Falls. But instead I remained on the leather club seat, wishing I could stay in the library, breathing in Katherine's scent, forever.

'May I make an observation?' she asked, leaning towards me. An errant dark curl flopped down on her white forehead. I had to use all my strength to resist pushing it off her face. 'I don't think you like what's happening right now. The barbecue, the engagement . . .'

My heart pounded. I searched her brown eyes. For the past week, I'd been trying desperately to hide my feelings. But had she seen me pausing outside the carriage house? Had she seen me run Mezzanotte to the forest when she and Damon explored the garden, desperate to get away from their laughter? Had she somehow managed to read my thoughts?

Katherine smiled ruefully. 'Poor, sweet, steadfast Stefan. Haven't you learned yet that rules are made to be broken? You can't make anyone happy – your father, Rosalyn, the Cartwrights – if you're not happy yourself.'

I cleared my throat, aching with the realization that this woman who I'd known for a matter of weeks understood me better than my own father . . . and my future wife . . . ever would.

Katherine slid off the chair and glanced at the volumes on Father's shelves. She took down a thick leather-bound book, *The Mysteries of Mystic Falls*. It was a volume I'd never seen before. A smile lit her rose-coloured lips, and she beckoned me to join her on my father's couch. I knew I shouldn't, but as if in a trance, I stood and crossed the room. I sank into the cool, cracked leather cushion next to her and just let go.

After all, who knew? Perhaps a few moments in her presence would be the balm I needed to break my melancholia.

CHAPTER
8

I'm not sure how long we stayed in the room together. The minutes ticked away on the grandfather clock in the corner, but all I was aware of was the rhythmic sound of Katherine's breath, the way the light caught her angular jaw, the quick flick of the page as we looked through the book. I was dimly conscious of the fact that I needed to leave, soon, but whenever I thought of the music and the dancing and the plates of fried chicken and Rosalyn, I found myself literally unable to move.

'You're not reading!' Katherine teased at one point, glancing up from *The Mysteries of Mystic Falls*.

'No, I'm not.'

'Why? Are you distracted?' She rose, her slender shoulders stretching as she reached up to place the book back on the shelf. She put it in the wrong spot, next to Father's world geography books.

'Here,' I murmured, reaching behind her to take the book and place it on the high shelf where it belonged. The smell of lemon and ginger surrounded me, making me feel wobbly and dizzy. She turned towards me. Our lips were mere inches apart, and suddenly the scent of her became nearly unbearable. Even though my head knew it was wrong, my heart screamed that I'd never be complete if I didn't kiss Katherine. I closed my eyes and leaned in until my lips grazed hers.

For a moment, it felt as though my entire life had clicked into place. I saw Katherine running barefoot in the fields behind the guest house, me chasing after her, our young son slung over my shoulder.

But then, entirely unbidden, an image of Penny, her throat torn out, floated through my mind. I pulled back instantly, as if struck by lightning.

'I'm sorry!' I said, leaning back and tripping against a small end table, stacked high with Father's volumes. They fell to the floor, the sound muffled by the Oriental rugs. My mouth tasted like iron. What had I just done? What if my father had come in, eager to open the humidor with Mr Cartwright? My brain whirled in horror.

'I have to . . . I have to go. I have to go find my fiancée.' Without a backward glance at Katherine and the stunned expression that was sure to be on her face, I fled the study and ran through the empty conservatory and towards the garden.

Twilight was just beginning to fall. Coaches were setting off with mothers and young children as well as cautious revellers who were afraid of the animal attacks. Now was when the liquor would flow, the band would play more loudly and girls would outdo themselves waltzing, intent to capture the eyes of a Confederate soldier from the nearby camp. I felt my breath returning to normal. No one knew where I'd been, much less what I had done.

I strode purposefully into the centre of the party, as if I'd simply been refilling my glass at the bar. I saw Damon sitting with other soldiers, playing a round of poker on the corner of the porch. Five girls were squeezed onto the porch swing, giggling and talking loudly. Father and Mr Cartwright were walking towards the labyrinth, each holding a whiskey and gesturing in an animated fashion, no doubt talking about the benefits of the Cartwright-Salvatore merger.

'Stefan!' I felt a hand clap my back. 'We were wondering where the guests of honour were. No respect for their elders,' Robert said jovially.

'Rosalyn's still not here?' I asked.

'You know how girls are. They have to look just right, especially if they're celebrating their impending marriage,' Robert said.

His words rang true, yet an inexplicable shiver of fear rushed down my spine.

Was it just me, or had the sun set remarkably quickly? The revellers on the lawn had changed to shadowy figures in the five minutes since I'd been outside, and I couldn't make out Damon within the group in the corner.

Leaving Robert behind, I elbowed my way past the party guests. It was odd for a girl to not show up at her own party. What if, somehow, she'd come into the house and she'd seen . . .

But that was impossible. The door had been closed, the shades drawn. I walked briskly towards the servants' quarters near the pond, where the servants were having their own party, to see if Rosalyn's coachman had arrived.

The moon reflected off the water, casting an eerie greenish glow on the rocks and willow trees surrounding the pond. The grass was wet with dew, and still trampled from the time when Damon, Katherine and I had played football there. The knee-high mist made me wish I were wearing my boots instead of my dress shoes.

I squinted. At the base of the willow tree, where Damon and I had spent hours climbing as children, was a shadowy lump on the ground, like a large, gnarled tree root. Only I didn't remember a tree root in that spot. I squinted again. For a moment, I wondered if it could be a pair of intertwined lovers, trying to escape prying eyes. I smiled despite myself. At least someone had found love at this party.

But then the clouds shifted, and a shaft of moonlight illuminated the tree – and the form beneath it. I realized with a sickening jolt that the shape wasn't two lovers in mid-embrace. It was Rosalyn, my betrothed, her throat torn out, her eyes half open, staring up at the tree branches as if they held the secret to a universe she no longer inhabited.

CHAPTER

9

It's difficult for me to describe the moments that followed.

I remember footfalls and shrieking and the servants praying outside their quarters. I remember staying on my knees, yelling out of horror and pity and fear. I remember Mr Cartwright pulling me back as Mrs Cartwright sank to her knees and keened loudly, like a wounded animal.

I remember seeing the police carriage. I remember Father and Damon wringing their hands and whispering about me, allies in trying to develop the best course for my care. I tried to talk, to tell them I was fine – I was, after all, alive. But I couldn't form the words.

At one point, Dr Janes hooked his arms under my armpits and dragged me to my feet. Slowly, men I didn't know surrounded me and dragged me to the porch of the servants' quarters. There, words were mumbled, and Cordelia was called for. 'I'm . . . I'm fine,' I said finally, embarrassed that so much attention was being paid to me when Rosalyn was the one who'd been killed.

'Shhh, now, Stefan,' Cordelia said, her leathery face creased with worry. She pressed her hands to my chest and muttered a prayer under her breath, then pulled a tiny vial from the voluminous folds of her skirt. She uncapped it and pressed it to my lips. 'Drink,' she urged as a liquid that tasted like liquorice ran down my throat.

'Katherine!' I whimpered. Then I clapped my hand over my own mouth, but not before a startled expression crossed Cordelia's face. Quickly, she dosed me with more of the liquorice-scented liquid. I dropped back to the hard steps of the porch, too tired to think any more.

'His brother is here somewhere,' Cordelia said, sounding as if she were speaking underwater. 'Fetch him.'

I heard the sound of footfalls and opened my eyes an instant later to see Damon standing above me. His face was white with shock.

'Will he be OK?' Damon asked, turning to Cordelia.

'I think . . .' Dr Janes began.

'He needs rest. Quiet. A dark room,' Cordelia said authoritatively.

Damon nodded.

'I'm . . . Rosalyn . . . I should have . . .' I began, even though I didn't know how to finish the sentence. Should have what? Should have gone looking for her far earlier, instead of spending my time kissing Katherine? Should have insisted on escorting her to the party?

'Shhh,' Damon whispered, hoisting me up. I managed to stand, shakily, beside him. From out of nowhere, Father appeared and held my other arm, and I haltingly managed to step off the porch and back to the house. Revellers stood on the grass, holding each other, and Sheriff Forbes called out for the militia to search in the woods. I felt Damon guiding me through the back door of the house and up the stairs before allowing me to collapse on my bed. I fell into the cotton sheets, and then I remember nothing but darkness.

The next morning I awoke to beams of sunlight scattered on the cherrywood floorboards of my bedroom.

'Good morning, brother.' Damon was sitting in the corner in the rocking chair, the one that used to belong to Great-grandfather. Our mother had rocked us in it when we were infants, singing songs to us as we went to sleep. Damon's eyes were red and bloodshot, and I wondered if he'd been sitting like that, watching me, all night.

'Rosalyn's dead?' I voiced it as a question, even though the answer was obvious.

'Yes.' Damon stood up, turning to the crystal pitcher on the walnut dresser. He poured water into a tumbler and held it out to me. I struggled to sit upright.

'No, stay,' Damon commanded with the authority of an army officer. I'd never heard him speak like that before. I fell back against the goose-down pillows and allowed him to bring the glass to my lips as if I were an infant. The cool, clear liquid slipped down my throat, and once again I thought back to last night.

'Did she suffer?' I asked, a painful series of images marching through my brain. While I'd been reciting Shakespeare, Rosalyn must have been planning her grand entrance. She must have been so excited to show off her dress, to have the younger girls gape at her ring, to have the older women take her off to a corner to discuss the particulars of her wedding night. I imagined her dashing across the lawn, then hearing footsteps behind her, only to turn and see flashing white teeth glistening in the moonlight. I shuddered.

Damon crossed over to the bed and put his hand on my shoulder. Suddenly the rush of terrifying images stopped. 'Death usually happens in less than a second. That was the case in the war, and I'm sure it was the same for your Rosalyn.' He settled back in his chair and rubbed his temple. 'They think it was a coyote. The war is bringing people east for battle, and they think the animals are following the blood trail.'

'Coyotes,' I said, my voice tripping on the second syllable. I hadn't heard the word before. It was just one more example of new phrases like *killed* and *a widower* that were about to be added to my vocabulary.

'Of course, there are those people, including Father, who think it was the work of demons.' Damon rolled his dark eyes. 'Just what our town needs. An epidemic of mass hysteria. And what kills me about *that* little rumour is that when people are convinced their town is under siege by some demonic force, they're not focusing on the fact that war is ripping apart our country. It's this head-in-the-sand mentality that I simply cannot understand.'

I nodded, not really listening, not able to view Rosalyn's death as part of some sort of argument against the war. As Damon continued to ramble, I lay back and closed my eyes. I visualized Rosalyn's face at the moment I found her. There, in the darkness, she'd looked different. Her eyes had been large and luminescent. As though she'd seen something terrible. As though she'd suffered horribly.

CHAPTER

10

September 4, 1864
Midnight. Too late to fall asleep, too early to be
awake. A candle burns on my nightstand, the
flickering shadows foreboding.

I am haunted already. Will I ever forgive myself for
not finding Rosalyn until it was too late? And why is
she – the one I vowed to forget – still on my mind?

My head is pounding. Cordelia is always at the
door, offering drinks, lozenges, powdered herbs. I take
them, like a recuperating child. Father and Damon
glance at me when they think I'm asleep. Do they
know of the nightmares?

I thought marriage was a fate worse than death. I
was wrong. I was wrong about so many things, too
many things, and all I can do is pray for forgiveness
and hope that somehow, somewhere, I can summon

strength from the depths of my existence to step firmly onto the path of the right again. I will do it. I must. For Rosalyn.

And for her.

Now I will blow out the candle and hope for sleep – like that of the dead – to engulf me quickly . . .

'Stefan! Time to get up!' my father called, slamming my bedroom door.

'What?' I struggled to sit, not sure what hour it was, or what day it was, or how much time had passed since Rosalyn's death. Day faded into night, and I could never really sleep, only doze into terrifying dreams. I wouldn't have eaten anything, except that Cordelia continued to come into my room with her concoctions, spoon-feeding them to me to ensure that they were eaten. She'd make fried chicken and okra and a thick mash of what she called *sufferer stew*, which she said would make me feel better.

She'd left another one, a drink this time, on my nightstand. I drank it quickly.

'Get ready. Alfred will help you prepare,' my father said.

'Get ready for what?' I asked, swinging my legs onto the floor. I hobbled to the mirror. I had stubble over my chin, and my tawny hair stood up on all ends. My eyes were red, and my nightshirt was hanging off my shoulders. I looked awful.

Father stood behind me, appraising my reflection.

'You'll pull yourself together. Today is Rosalyn's funeral, and it's important to me and the Cartwrights that we are there. We want to show everyone that we must band together against the evil that's scourging our town.'

While Father prattled on about demons, I thought about facing the Cartwrights for the first time. I still felt horribly guilty. I couldn't help thinking that the attack wouldn't have happened if I'd been waiting for Rosalyn on the porch, instead of lingering in the study with Katherine. If I'd been outside, waiting for Rosalyn, I would have seen her walking from the fields in her pink dress. Maybe I could have faced death with her, too, and she wouldn't have had to confront that nightmarish animal alone. I may not have loved Rosalyn, but I couldn't forgive myself for not being there to save her.

'Well, come on,' Father said impatiently as Alfred walked in, holding a white linen shirt and a double-breasted black suit. I blanched. It was the suit I'd have worn at my wedding – and the church where we were mourning Rosalyn was to have been the site of the ceremony establishing our union. Still, I managed to change into the suit, allowed Alfred to help me shave, since my hands were so shaky, and emerged an hour later ready to do what I had to do.

I kept my eyes down as I followed Father and Damon to the carriage. Father sat up front, next to Alfred, while Damon sat in the back with me.

'How are you, brother?' Damon asked above the

familiar clip-clop of Duke's and Jake's hooves down Willow Creek Road.

'Not very well,' I said formally, a stiff lump in my throat.

Damon put a hand on my shoulder. The magpies chattered, the bees buzzed and the sun cast a golden glow on the trees. The entire coach smelled like ginger, and I felt my stomach heave. It was the smell of guilt over lusting after a woman who was never to be – *could* never be – my wife.

'Your first death, the first one you witness, changes you,' Damon said finally, as the coach pulled up to the white clapboard church. The church bells were ringing, and every business in town was closed for the day. 'But perhaps it can change you for the better.'

'Maybe,' I said as I descended from the coach. But I didn't see how.

We reached the door as Dr Janes hobbled into the church, his cane in one hand and a flask of whiskey in another. Pearl and Anna were sitting together, and Jonathan Gilbert sat behind them, his elbows perched on the edge of Pearl's pew, just inches from her shoulder.

Sheriff Forbes was in his usual place in the second pew, glaring at the cluster of rouged women from the tavern who had come to pay their respects. At the edge of their circle was Alice, the barmaid, cooling herself with a silk fan.

Calvin Bailey, the organist, was playing an

adaptation of Mozart's *Requiem*, but he seemed to hit a sour note every few chords. In the front pew, Mr Cartwright stared straight ahead, while Mrs Cartwright sobbed and occasionally blew her nose into a lace handkerchief. At the front of the church, a closed oak casket was covered with flowers. Wordlessly, I walked to the casket and knelt down in front of it.

'I'm so sorry,' I whispered, touching the casket, which felt cold and hard. Unbidden, images of my betrothed popped up in my mind: Rosalyn giggling over her new puppy, giddily discussing flower combinations for our wedding, risking the wrath of her maid by planting a covert kiss on my cheek at the end of one visit. I moved my hands off the casket and put them together, as if in prayer. 'I hope that you and Penny have found each other in Heaven.' I leaned down, letting my lips graze the casket. I wanted her to know, wherever she was, that I would have learned to love her. 'Goodbye.'

I turned to take my seat and stopped short. Right behind me was Katherine. She was wearing a dark-blue cotton dress that stood out in the sea of black crepe that filled the pews.

'I'm so sorry for your loss,' Katherine said, touching my arm. I flinched and drew my arm back. How dare she touch me so familiarly in public? Didn't she *realize* that if we hadn't been carrying on at the barbecue in the first place, the tragedy might never have happened?

Concern registered in her dark eyes. 'I know how hard this must be for you,' she said. 'Please let me know if you need anything.'

I immediately felt a wave of guilt for assuming she was doing anything other than showing sympathy. After all, her parents had died. She was just a young girl, reaching out to offer her support. She looked so sad that for one wild second, I was tempted to cross the aisle and comfort her.

'Thank you,' I said instead, sucking in my stale breath and walking back to the pew. I slid next to Damon, who had his hands crossed piously over a Bible. I noticed his eyes flick up as Katherine briefly knelt down by the coffin. I followed his gaze, noticing the way several curls had escaped from beneath her hat and were curling around the ornate clasp on her blue necklace.

A few minutes later, the *Requiem* ended, and Pastor Collins strode up to the pulpit. 'We're here to celebrate a life cut far too short. There is evil among us, and we will mourn this death, but we will also draw strength from this death . . .' he intoned.

I covertly glanced across the aisle at Katherine. Her servant, Emily, was sitting next to her on one side and Pearl on the other. Katherine's hands were folded as if in prayer. She turned slightly, as if to look at me. I forced myself to look away before our eyes could meet. I would not dishonour Rosalyn by thinking of Katherine.

I gazed up at the unfinished, steepled beams of the

church. *I'm sorry*, I thought, sending the message upward and hoping that Rosalyn, wherever she was, heard it.

CHAPTER
11

The mist rose up around my feet as I walked towards the willow tree. The sun was quickly setting, but I could still make out a shadowy figure nestled between the roots.

I glanced again. It was Rosalyn, her party dress shimmering in the weak light. Bile rose in my throat. How could she be here? She was buried, her body six feet under ground at the Mystic Falls cemetery.

As I walked closer, steeling my courage and grasping the knife in my pocket, I noticed her lifeless eyes reflecting the verdant leaves above. Her dark curls stuck to her clammy forehead. And her neck wasn't torn out at all. Instead, her neck displayed only two neat little holes, the size of shodding nails. As if guided by an unseen hand, I fell to my knees next to her body.

'I'm sorry,' I whispered, staring at the cracked earth below. Then I raised my eyes and froze in horror. Because it wasn't Rosalyn's body at all.

It was Katherine's.

A small smile curved her rosebud lips, as if she were simply dreaming.

I fought the urge to scream. I would not let Katherine die! But as I reached towards her wounds, she sat straight up. Her visage morphed, her dark curls faded to blonde, and her eyes glowed red.

I started backwards.

'It's your fault!' The words cut through the still night, the tone hollow and otherworldly. The voice belonged neither to Katherine nor Rosalyn – but to a demon.

I screamed, gripping my penknife and slicing it into the night air. The demon lunged forward and clutched my neck. It lowered its sharpened canines to my skin, and everything faded to black . . .

I woke up in a cold sweat, sitting upright. A crow cawed outside; in the distance I could hear children playing. Sunbeams were dappled along my white bedspread, and a dinner tray was sitting on my desk. It was daylight. I was in my own bed.

A dream. I remembered the funeral, the ride from the church, my exhaustion as I climbed the stairs to my bedroom. It had just been a dream, a product of too much emotion and stimulation today. *A dream*, I reminded myself again, willing my heart to stop pounding. I took a long gulp of water straight from the pitcher on the nightstand. My brain slowly stilled, but my heart continued to race and my hands still felt clammy. Because it *wasn't* a dream, or at least not like any dream I'd ever had before. It was as if demons were invading my mind, and I was no longer sure what was real or what thoughts to trust.

I stood up, trying to shake off the nightmare, and wandered downstairs. I took the back steps so as not to cross paths with Cordelia in the kitchen. She'd been taking good care of me, just as when I had been a child in mourning for my mother, but something about her watchful gaze made me nervous. I knew she'd heard me call out for Katherine, and I fervently hoped she wasn't telling tales to the servants.

I walked into Father's study and glanced at his shelves, finding myself drawn yet again to the Shakespeare section. Saturday seemed like a lifetime ago. Still, the candle in the silver candlestick holder was exactly where Katherine and I had left it, and *The Mysteries of Mystic Falls* was still on the chair. If I closed my eyes, I could almost smell lemon.

I shook that thought away and hastily picked out a volume of *Macbeth*, a play about jealousy and love and betrayal and death, which suited my mood perfectly.

I forced myself to sit on the leather club chair and glance at the words, forced myself to turn the pages. Maybe that's what I needed in order to proceed with the rest of my life. If I just kept forcing myself to take action, maybe I'd finally get over the guilt and sadness and fear I'd been carrying with me since Rosalyn's death.

Just then, I heard a knock on the door.

'Father's not here,' I called, hoping whoever it was would go away.

'Sir Stefan?' Alfred's voice called. 'It's a visitor.'

'No, thank you,' I replied. It was probably Sheriff Forbes again. He'd already come by four or five times, speaking to Damon and Father. So far I'd managed to beg off the visits. I couldn't stand the thought of telling him – telling anyone – where I'd been at the time of the attack.

'The visitor is quite insistent,' Alfred called.

'So are you,' I muttered under my breath as I strode to the door and opened it.

'She's in the sitting room,' Alfred said, turning on his heel.

'Wait!' I said. *She*. Could it be . . . Katherine? My heart quickened despite itself.

'Sir?' Alfred asked, mid-step.

'I'll be there.'

Frantically, I splashed water from the basin in the corner on my face and used my hands to smooth my hair back from my forehead. My eyes still looked hooded, and tiny vessels had broken, reddening the whites, but there was nothing more I could do to make me look, let alone feel, more like myself.

I strode purposefully into the parlour. For an instant, my heart fell with disappointment. Instead of Katherine, sitting on the red velvet wingback chair in the corner was her maid, Emily. She had a basket of flowers on her lap and held a daisy to her nose, as if she didn't have a care in the world.

'Hello,' I said formally, already trying to come up with a way to politely excuse myself.

'Mr Salvatore.' Emily stood up and half-curtseyed. She wore a simple white eyelet dress and bonnet, and her dark skin was smooth and unlined. 'My mistress and I join you in your sorrows. She asked that I give you this,' she said, proffering the basket towards me.

'Thank you,' I said, taking the basket. I absentmindedly put a sprig of lilac to my nose and inhaled.

'I'd use these in your healing, rather than Cordelia's concoctions,' Emily said.

'How did you know about that?' I wondered.

'Servants talk. But I fear that whatever Cordelia's feeding you may be doing you more harm than good.' She plucked a few blossoms from the basket, twining them into a bouquet. 'Daisies, magnolias and bleeding heart will help you heal.'

'And pansies for thoughts?' I asked, remembering a quote from Shakespeare's *Hamlet*. As soon as I said it, I realized it was a foolish statement. How would an uneducated servant girl possibly know what I was speaking of?

But Emily simply smiled. 'No pansies, although my mistress did mention your love of Shakespeare.' She reached into the basket and broke off a sprig of lilac, which she then pushed gently into my buttonhole.

I held the basket up and inhaled. It smelled like flowers, but there was something else: the intoxicating aroma that I'd only experienced when I was near Katherine. I inhaled again, feeling the confusion and darkness of the past few days slowly fade.

'I know everything's very strange right now,' Emily said, breaking my reverie. 'But my mistress only wishes the best for you.' She nodded towards the couch, as if inviting me to sit down. Obediently, I sat and stared at her. She was remarkably beautiful and carried herself with a type of grace I'd never seen before. Her movements and manners were so deliberate that watching her was like watching a painting come to life.

'She would like to see you,' Emily said after a moment.

The second the words left her lips, I realized that could never be. As I sat there, in the daylight of the parlour, with another person rather than being lost in my own thoughts, everything clicked into focus. I was a widower, and my duty now was to mourn Rosalyn, not to mourn my schoolboy fantasy of love with Katherine. Besides, Katherine was a beautiful orphan with no friends or relations. It would never work – could never work.

'I did see her. At Rosalyn's . . . at the funeral,' I said stiffly.

'That's hardly a social call,' Emily pointed out. 'She'd like to see you. Somewhere private. When you're ready,' she added quickly.

I knew what I had to say, what the only proper thing *to* say was, but the words were hard to form. 'I will see, but in my current condition, I'm afraid I'm probably not in the best mood to go walking. Please send your mistress my regrets, although she will not want for company. I know my brother will go wherever she wishes,' I said, the words heavy on my tongue.

'Yes. She is quite fond of Damon.' Emily gathered her skirts and stood up. I stood up as well and felt, even though I towered a head taller, that she was somehow more powerful than me. It was an odd yet not altogether unpleasant feeling. 'But you can't argue with true love.'

With that she swept out the door and across the grounds, the daisy in her hair scattering its petals into the wind.

CHAPTER

12

I'm not sure if it was the fresh air or the flowers Emily had brought me, but I slept soundly that night. The next morning I woke up to bright sunlight in my chambers and, for the first time since Rosalyn's death, didn't bother to drink the concoction Cordelia had left on my nightstand. The smell of cinnamon and eggs floated up from the kitchen, and I heard the snort of the horses as Alfred hitched them outside. For a second, I felt a thrill of possibility and the nascent bud of happiness.

'Stefan!' my father boomed on the other side of the door, rapping three times with his walking stick or riding crop. Just like that, I remembered all that had transpired in the past week, and my malaise returned.

I remained silent, hoping he'd simply go away. But

instead he swung the door open. He was wearing his riding breeches and carried his black riding crop, a smile on his face and a sprig of a violet flower in his lapel. It was neither pretty nor fragrant; in fact, it looked like one of the herbs Cordelia grew down by the servants' quarters.

'We're going riding,' Father announced as he swung open the shutters. I shaded my eyes against the glare. Was the world always so bright? 'This chamber needs to be cleaned and you, my boy, need sun.'

'But I should really attend to my studies,' I said, gesturing limply to the volume of *Macbeth* open on my desk.

Father took the book and closed it with a definitive clap. 'I need to speak to you and Damon, away from any prying ears.' He glanced suspiciously around the chambers. I followed his gaze but saw nothing except for a collection of dirty dishes that Cordelia hadn't yet cleared.

As if on cue, Damon strode into the room, wearing a pair of mustard-coloured breeches and his grey Confederate coat. 'Father!' Damon rolled his eyes. 'Don't tell me you're on about that demon nonsense again.'

'It's not nonsense!' Father roared. 'Stefan, I'll see you and your brother at the stable,' he said, turning on his heel and striding out. Damon shook his head, then followed him, leaving me to change.

I put on my full riding costume – a grey waistcoat and brown breeches – and sighed, not sure I had enough strength to ride or to endure another marathon bickering session between my father and brother. When I opened the door, I found Damon standing at the bottom of the curved staircase, waiting.

'Feeling better, brother?' he asked as we walked out the door and across the lawn together.

I nodded, even as I noticed the spot under the willow tree where I'd found Rosalyn. The grass was long and bright green, and squirrels were darting around the tree's gnarled trunk. Sparrows chirped, and the drooping branches of the weeping willow looked lush and full of promise. There was no sign that anything had been amiss.

I breathed a sigh of relief when we reached the stable, inhaling the familiar, loved scent of well-oiled leather and sawdust. 'Hi, girl,' I whispered into Mezzanotte's velvety ear. She whinnied in appreciation. Her coat was silky-smooth, even more so than the last time I'd brushed it. 'Sorry I haven't come to visit you, but it looks like my brother's taken good care of you.'

'Actually, Katherine's taken a shine to her. Which is too bad for her own horses.' Damon smiled fondly as he jerked his chin to two coal-black mares in the corner. Indeed, they were stamping their feet and staring at the ground dejectedly, as if to express just how ignored and lonely they were.

'You've been spending quite a bit of time with Katherine,' I said finally. It was a statement, not a question. Of course he had been. Damon always had an ease around women. I knew he *knew* women, especially after his year in the Confederate army. He'd told me stories about some of the women he'd met in cities like Atlanta and Lexington that had made me blush. Did he *know* Katherine?

'I have been,' Damon said, swinging his leg over the back of his horse, Jake. He didn't elaborate.

'Ready, boys?' Father called, his horse impatiently stamping its feet. I nodded and fell into stride behind Damon and Father as we headed to the Wickery Bridge, all the way on the other end of the property.

We crossed the bridge and continued on into the forest. I blinked in relief. The sunlight had been too bright. I much preferred the dark shadows of the trees. The woods were cool, with wet leaves covering the forest floor, even though there hadn't been a rainstorm recently. The leaves were so thick, you could see only slight patches of blue sky, and occasionally I'd hear the rustle of a raccoon or badger in the underbrush. I tried not to think of the animal noises as coming from the beast that had attacked Rosalyn.

We continued riding into the forest until we reached the clearing. Father abruptly stopped and hitched his horse to a birch tree. I obediently hitched Mezzanotte to a tree and glanced around. The clearing was marked by a collection of rocks set up in a rough circle, above which the trees parted to provide a natural window to the sky. I hadn't been there in ages, not since before Damon went away. When we were boys, we used to play illicit card games here with the other fellows in town. Everyone knew the clearing was the place boys came to gamble, girls came to gossip and everyone came to spill their secrets. If Father really meant to keep our conversation quiet, he'd have been better off taking us to the tavern to talk.

'We're in trouble,' Father said without preamble, glancing up at the sky. I followed his gaze, expecting to see a fast-moving summer storm. Instead, the sky was spotless and blue. I found no solace in this beautiful day. I was still haunted by Rosalyn's lifeless eyes.

'We're *not*, Father,' Damon said thickly. 'You know who's in trouble? All of the soldiers fighting this godforsaken war for this cause you've made me try to believe in. The problem is the war and your incessant need to find conflict everywhere you turn.' Damon angrily stomped his feet, reminding me so much of Mezzanotte that I stifled the urge to laugh.

'I will *not* have you talk back to me!' Father said, shaking his fist at Damon. I glanced back and forth at the two of them, as though I were watching a tennis match. Damon towered over Father's sloping shoulders, and for the first time I realized that Father was getting old.

Damon put his hands on his hips. 'Then talk. Let's hear what you have to say.'

I expected Father to shout, but instead he crossed to one of the rocks, his knees creaking as he bent to sit. 'You want to know why I left Italy? I left it for you. For my future children. I knew I wanted my sons to grow and marry and have children on land I owned and land I loved. And I *do* love this land, and I will not watch it be destroyed by demons,' Father said, flinging his hands wildly. I stepped back, and Mezzanotte whinnied a long, plaintive note. 'Demons,' he repeated, as if to prove his point.

'Demons?' Damon snorted. 'More like big dogs. Don't you see it's talk like this that will make you lose everything? You say you want a good life for us, but you're always deciding how we'll live that life. You made me go to war and made Stefan get engaged, and now you're making us believe your fairy tales,' he yelled in frustration.

I glanced at Father guiltily. I didn't want him to know I hadn't loved Rosalyn. But Father didn't look at me. He was too busy glowering at Damon.

'All I wanted was for my boys to have the best. I know what we're facing, and I do not have time for your schoolboy arguments. I am not telling tales right now.' Father glanced back at me, and I forced myself to look into his dark eyes. 'Please understand. There are demons who walk among us. They existed in the old country, too. They walked the same earth, talked like humans. But they wouldn't drink like humans.'

'Well, if they don't drink wine, that would be a blessing, wouldn't it?' Damon asked sarcastically. I stiffened. I remembered all the times after Mother had died that Father would drink too much wine or whiskey, lock himself in the study, then mumble late into the night about ghosts or demons.

'Damon!' Father said, his voice even sharper than my brother's. 'I will ignore your impudence. But I will *not* have you ignore me. Listen to me, Stefan.' Father turned towards me. 'What you saw happen to your young Rosalyn wasn't natural. It wasn't one of Damon's *coyotes*,' Father said, practically spitting out the word. 'It was *un vampiro*. They were in the old country, and now they're here,' Father said, screwing up his florid face. 'And they are doing harm. They're feeding on us. And we need to stop it.'

'What do you mean?' I asked nervously, any trace of exhaustion or dizziness gone. All I felt was fear. I thought back to Rosalyn, but this time, instead of remembering her eyes, I remembered the blood on her throat, having flowed from the two precise circles on the side of her neck. I touched my own neck, feeling the pulse of blood beneath my skin. The rush below my fingers sped up as I felt my heart skip a beat. Could Father be . . . right?

'Father means that he's been spending too much time listening to the church ladies tell their tales. Father, this is a story that would be told to scare a child. And not a very clever one. Everything you're saying is nonsense.' Damon shook his head and angrily stood from his perch on the tree stump. 'I will not sit around and be told ghost stories.' With that, he turned on his gold-buttoned boot and swung his foot up over Jake's back, gazing down at Father, as if daring him to say one more thing.

'Mark my words,' Father said, taking a step closer to me. 'Vampires are among us. They look like us and can live among us, but they are not who we are. They drink blood. It is their elixir of life. They do not have souls, and they never die. They are forever immortal.'

The word *immortal* made me suck in my breath. The wind changed, and the leaves began rustling. I shivered. 'Vampires,' I repeated slowly. I'd heard the word once before, when Damon and I were schoolchildren and used to gather on the Wickery Bridge, trying to scare our friends. One boy had told us of seeing a figure kneeling down in the woods, feasting on the neck of a deer. The boy told us he had screamed and the figure had turned to him with hell-red eyes, blood dripping from long, sharp teeth. *A vampire*, he said with conviction, glancing around the circle to see if he'd impressed any of us. But because he'd been pale and scrawny and not any good at shooting, we'd laughed and mocked him mercilessly. He and his family had moved to Richmond the next year.

'Well, I'd take vampires over an insane father,' Damon said, kicking Jake's flanks and riding off into the sunset. I turned towards Father, expecting an angry tirade. But Father simply shook his head.

'Do you believe me, son?' he asked.

I nodded, even though I wasn't sure what I believed. All I knew was that somehow, in the past week, the whole world had changed, and I wasn't sure where I fitted in any more.

'Good.' Father nodded as we rode out of the forest and onto the bridge. 'We must be careful. It seems the war has awakened the vampires. It's as if they can smell blood.'

The word *blood* echoed in my mind as we directed our horses to walk away from the cemetery and towards the shortcut through the fields that would lead to the pond. In the distance, I could see the sun reflecting on the pond's surface. No one would ever imagine this verdant, rolling land as being a place where demons walked. Demons, if they existed at all, belonged in the old country, amid the decrepit churches and castles Father had grown up with. All the words he said were familiar, but they sounded so strange in the place where he was saying them.

Father glanced around as if to make sure no one was hiding in the bushes near the bridge. The horses were walking alongside the graveyard now, the headstones bright and imposing in the warm summer light. 'Blood is what they feed on. It gives them power.'

'But then . . .' I said, as the information whirled in my brain. 'If they are immortal, then how are we to . . .'

'Kill them?' Father asked, finishing my thought. He pulled the reins on his horse. 'There are methods. I've been learning. I've heard there's a priest in Richmond who can try to exorcize them, but then people in town know . . . some things,' he finished.

'Jonathan Gilbert and Sheriff Forbes and I have discussed some preliminary measures.'

'If there's anything I can do . . .' I offered finally, unsure what to say.

'Of course,' Father said brusquely. 'I expect you to be part of our committee. For starters, I've been talking to Cordelia. She knows her herbs, and she says there's a plant called vervain.' Father's hand fluttered to the flower on his lapel. 'We will come up with a plan. And we will prevail. Because while they may have immortality, we have God on our side. It is kill or be killed. Do you understand me, boy? This is the war you're being drafted to fight.'

I nodded, feeling the full weight of the responsibility on my shoulders. Maybe *this* was what I was meant to be doing: not getting married or going off to war, but fighting an unnatural evil. I met Father's gaze.

'I'll do whatever you want,' I said. 'Anything.'

The last thing I saw before I galloped back to the stable was the huge grin on Father's face. 'I knew you would, son. You are a true Salvatore.'

CHAPTER

13

I walked back to my room, unsure what to think. *Vampiros*. Vampires. The word sounded wrong, no matter what language it was in. Coyotes. *That* was a word that made sense. After all, a coyote was just like a wolf, a wild animal drawn to the confusing tangle of the deep Virginia woods. If Rosalyn was killed by a coyote, it would be tragic, but understandable. But for Rosalyn to be killed by a *demon*?

I laughed, the sound coming out like a short bark as I strode into my bedroom and sat with my head in my hands. My headache had returned with renewed vigour, and I remembered Emily's request that I not eat Cordelia's cooking. On top of everything else, it seemed the servants were turning on each other.

Suddenly, I heard three soft raps on the door. The sound was so slight it might have been the wind, which had shown no sign of stopping since we got back from the woods.

'Hello?' I called hesitantly.

The raps started again, more insistently this time. On the other side of the room, the cotton curtains blew violently in the wind.

'Alfred?' I called, the hairs on the back of my neck standing up. Father's tale had definitely affected me. 'I won't be needing dinner,' I called loudly.

I grabbed a letter opener from my desk and held it behind my back as I headed cautiously towards the door. But just as I placed my hand on the doorknob, the door began to swing inwards.

'This isn't funny!' I called, half hysterical, when all of a sudden, a figure in pale blue slipped into the room.

Katherine.

'Good, because humour has never been one of my strong points,' Katherine said, her smile revealing her straight white teeth.

'I'm sorry.' I blushed and hastily dropped the letter opener onto the desk. 'I'm just . . .'

'You're still recovering.' Katherine's brown eyes locked with my own. 'I'm sorry to startle you.' She sat down on the centre of my bed, pulling her knees up to her chest. 'Your brother's worried about you.'

'Oh . . .' I stammered. I couldn't believe that Katherine Pierce had come into my bedroom and was sitting on my bed, as if it were perfectly normal. No woman, except my mother and Cordelia, had ever been in my sleeping chambers. I was suddenly embarrassed by my muddy boots in one corner, the pile of china dishes in another and the Shakespeare volume still open on the desk.

'Do you want to know a secret?' Katherine asked.

I stood at the door, clutching the brass doorknob. 'Maybe?' I asked hesitantly.

'Come closer and I'll tell you.' She beckoned me with her finger. Townspeople were scandalized if a couple went walking to the Wickery Bridge without a chaperone. But here Katherine was without a chaperone – or stockings, for that matter – perched on my bed, asking me to join her there.

There was no way I could resist that.

I gingerly sat on the edge of the bed. Immediately she flipped onto her hands and knees and crawled over to me. Pushing her hair over one shoulder, she cupped my ear with her hand.

'My secret is that I've been worried about you, too,' she whispered.

Her breath was unnaturally cold against my cheek. My leg muscles twitched. I knew I should demand that she leave, right away. But instead I inched closer to her.

'Really?' I whispered.

'Yes,' Katherine murmured, looking deep into my eyes. 'You need to forget Rosalyn.'

I shivered and glanced away from her dark-brown eyes towards the window, watching a fast-moving summer storm sweep in.

Katherine took my chin in her ice-cold hands and

turned my eyes back to hers. 'Rosalyn is dead,' she continued, her face full of sorrow and kindness. 'But you aren't. Rosalyn wouldn't have wanted you to shut yourself away like a criminal. No one would want that for their betrothed, don't you agree?'

I nodded slowly. Even though Damon had told me the same thing, the words made infinitely more sense when coming from Katherine's mouth.

Her lips curved in a small smile. 'You'll find happiness again,' she said. 'I want to help you. But you have to let me, sweet Stefan.' Katherine laid her hand against my forehead. I felt a surge of heat and ice converging at my temple. I flinched from the force of it, disappointment welling in my chest as her hand dropped back into her lap.

'Are those the flowers I picked for you?' she asked suddenly, looking across the room. 'You've shoved them into the corner without any light!'

'I'm sorry,' I said.

She imperiously swung her legs off the bed and bent to take the basket from under my desk. She drew the shades, then stared at me, her arms crossed over her chest. My breath caught in my throat. Her light-blue crepe dress highlighted her tiny waist, and her necklace lay at the hollow of her neck. She was undeniably beautiful.

She plucked a daisy from the bunch, removing the petals one by one. 'Yesterday I saw a servant child play a silly game – *he loves me, he loves me not.*' She laughed, but then her smile abruptly turned solemn.

'What do you think the answer would be?'

And suddenly, she stood above me, her hands on my shoulders. I inhaled her scent of ginger and lemon, unsure what to say, knowing only that I wanted to feel her hands on my shoulders forever. 'Would the answer be he loves me . . . or he loves me not?' Katherine asked, leaning towards me. My body began quivering with a desire I didn't know I possessed. My lips were mere inches away from hers.

'What's the answer?' she asked, biting her lip in the impression of a shy maiden. I laughed despite myself. I felt as if I were watching the scene unfold, powerless to stop what I was about to do. I knew this was wrong. Sinful. But how could it be sinful if every fibre of my being wanted it more than anything? Rosalyn was dead. Katherine was alive. And I was alive, too, and I needed to start acting like it.

If what Father said was true, and I was about to fight the battle of my life between good and evil, then I needed to learn to have confidence in myself and my choices. I needed to stop thinking and start believing in myself, in my convictions, in my desires.

'Do you really need me to answer?' I asked, reaching for her waist. I grabbed her and pulled her onto the bed with a strength I didn't know I possessed. She shrieked in delight and tumbled onto the bed next to me. Her breath was sweet, and her hands were cold and holding mine, and suddenly, nothing else – not Rosalyn, not my father's demons, not even Damon – mattered.

CHAPTER

14

I woke the next morning and stretched my arms outwards, dejected when I touched nothing but goose-down pillows. A slight indentation in the mattress next to me was the only proof that what had happened had been real, and not one of the fever dreams I'd been having since Rosalyn's death.

Of course, I couldn't expect Katherine to have spent the night with me. Not with her maid waiting at the carriage house, and not with the way the servants talked. She'd told me herself that this had to be our secret, that she couldn't risk ruining her reputation. Not that she had to worry about that. I wanted us to have our own secret world, together.

I wondered when she'd slipped away, remembering the feeling of her in my arms, a warmth and lightness I'd never felt before. I felt whole, and at peace, and the thought of Rosalyn was just a vague memory, a character in an unpleasant story that I'd simply put out of my mind.

Now my mind was consumed with thoughts of Katherine: how she pulled the curtains closed as the summer storm pelted hail on the windows, how she'd allowed my hands to explore her exquisite body. At one point, I was caressing her neck when my hands fell on the clasp of the ornate blue cameo necklace she always wore. I began to unclasp it when Katherine had roughly pushed me away.

'Don't!' she'd said sharply, her hands flying to the clasp, making sure nothing had been disturbed. But then, once she patted the charm into place on the hollow of her neck, she'd resumed kissing me.

I blushed as I remembered all the other places she *did* allow me to touch.

I swung my legs out of bed, walked towards the hand basin, and splashed water on my face. I looked in the mirror and smiled. The dark circles were gone from my eyes, and it no longer felt like an effort to walk from one side of the room to the other. I changed into my waistcoat and dark-blue breeches and left the chambers humming.

'Sir?' Alfred asked on the stairs. He was holding a silver-domed platter – my breakfast. My lip curled in disgust. How could I have lain in bed for an entire week when there was a whole *world* to discover with Katherine?

'I'm quite well, thank you, Alfred,' I said as I took

the stairs two at a time. The storm from last night had disappeared as quickly as it came. In the sunroom, the early-morning light was sparkling through the floor-to-ceiling windows, and the table was decorated with freshly-cut daisies. Damon was already there, drinking a mug of coffee while flipping through the morning paper from Richmond.

'Hello, brother!' Damon said, holding up his coffee mug as if he were toasting me. 'My, you look well. Did our afternoon ride do you some good, after all?'

I nodded and sat opposite him, glancing at the headlines on the paper. The Union had taken Fort Morgan. I wondered where exactly that was.

'I don't know why we even get the paper. It's not like Father cares about anything except the stories he makes up in his head,' Damon said disgustedly.

'If you hate it here so much, why don't you just leave?' I asked, suddenly annoyed with his constant grumbling. Maybe it *would* be better if he were gone, so that Father wouldn't be so frustrated. An odious voice in the back of my mind silently added, *And so I don't have to think about you and Katherine, swinging on the porch swing together*.

Damon raised an eyebrow. 'Well, I'd be remiss if I didn't say things were *interesting* here.' His lips curved in a private sort of smile that made me suddenly want to grab his shoulders and shake him.

The force of my emotions surprised me, so much so that I had to sit down and shove into my mouth a muffin from the overflowing basket on the table. I'd never felt jealous of my brother before, but suddenly I was dying to know: had Katherine ever snuck up to his bedroom? *She couldn't have.* Last night, she'd seemed so nervous about getting caught, having me promise over and over again that I'd never breathe a word to anybody about what we'd done.

Betsy, the cook, came in, her arms laden with plates of grits, bacon and eggs. My stomach rumbled, and I realized I was starving. I quickly tucked in, revelling in the saltiness of the eggs combined with the sweet bitterness of my coffee. It was as if I'd never tasted breakfast before and my senses were finally awakened. I sighed in contentment, and Damon looked up in amusement.

'I *knew* all you needed was some fresh air and good food,' he said.

And Katherine, I thought.

'Now let's go outside and cause some trouble.' Damon smiled wickedly. 'Father's in his study, doing his demon studies. Do you know he even has Robert in on it?' Damon shook his head in disgust.

I sighed. While I didn't necessarily believe all the discussion about demons, I did respect Father enough to not make fun of his thoughts. It made me feel vaguely disloyal to hear Damon's dismissal of him.

'I'm sorry, brother.' Damon shook his head and scraped his chair back against the slate floor. 'I know you don't like it when Father and I fight.' He walked over to me, pulling out my chair from under me, almost causing me to fall. I scrambled to my feet and good-naturedly shoved him back.

'That's better!' he called with glee. 'Now, let's go!' He ran out of the back door, letting it slam shut. Cordelia used to scream at us for that offence as children, and I laughed when I heard her familiar groan from the kitchen. I ran towards the centre of the lawn, where Damon had unearthed the oval ball we'd been tossing two weeks before.

'Here, brother! Catch!' Damon panted, and I turned and leapt into the air, just in time to catch the pigskin in my arms. I pulled it tightly to my chest and began running towards the stable, the wind whipping my face.

'You boys!' a voice called, stopping me in my tracks. Katherine was standing on the porch of the carriage house, wearing a simple, cream-coloured muslin dress and looking so innocent and sweet that I couldn't believe that what happened last night wasn't a dream. 'Burning off excess energy?'

I sheepishly turned around and walked towards the porch.

'Playing catch!' I explained, hastily throwing the ball to Damon.

Katherine reached behind her, braiding her curls down the back of her neck. I had a sudden fear that she thought we were tiresome with our childish game and that she'd come out here to scold us for waking her so early. But she simply smiled as she settled on the porch swing.

'Are you ready to play?' Damon called from his

position on the lawn. He held the ball far back behind his head as if he were about to throw it towards her.

'Absolutely *not.*' Katherine wrinkled her nose. 'Once was enough. Besides, I feel people who need props for their games and sports are lacking in imagination.'

'Stefan has imagination.' Damon smirked. 'You should hear him read poetry. He's like a troubadour.' He dropped the ball and ran over to the porch.

'Damon has imagination too. You should see the imaginative way he plays cards,' I teased as I reached the steps of the porch.

Katherine nodded at me as I bowed to her but didn't make any other effort to greet me. I stepped back, momentarily stung. Why hadn't she at least given me her hand to kiss? Hadn't last night meant anything to her?

'I *am* imaginative, especially when I have a muse.' Damon winked at Katherine, then stepped in front of me to grab her hand. He brought it to his lips, and my stomach churned.

'Thank you,' she said, standing up and walking down the porch steps, her simple skirts swishing down the stairs. With her hair pulled back from her eyes, she reminded me of an angel. She gave me a secret smile, and finally I relaxed.

'It's beautiful here,' Katherine said, spreading her arms as if blessing the entire estate. 'Will you show me around?' she asked, turning and glancing first at Damon, then at me, then back at Damon again. 'I've lived here for more than two weeks, and I've barely seen *anything* besides my bedchambers and the gardens. I want to see something new. Something secret!'

'We have a maze,' I said stupidly. Damon elbowed me in the ribs. Not like *he* had anything better to say.

'I know,' Katherine said. 'Damon showed me.'

My stomach fell at the reminder of how much time the two of them had spent together in the week I was in my sickbed. And if he'd shown her the maze . . .

But I pushed the thought out of my head as best I could. Damon had always told me about all the women he'd kissed, ever since we were thirteen and he and Amelia Hawke had kissed on the Wickery Bridge. If he had kissed Katherine, I would have heard about it.

'I'd love to see it again,' she said, clapping her hands together as if I'd just told her the most interesting news in the world. 'Will you both escort me?' she asked hopefully, glancing at us.

'Of course,' we said at the same time.

'Oh, wonderful! I must tell Emily.' Katherine dashed inside, leaving us standing on opposite ends of the stairs.

'She's quite a woman, isn't she?' Damon asked.

'She is,' I said shortly. Before I could say anything else, Katherine came bounding down the stairs, holding a sun umbrella in one hand.

'I'm ready for our adventure!' she cried, handing me her parasol, an expectant look on her face. I hooked it over the crook of my arm, while she linked arms with Damon. I walked a few feet behind, watching the easy way their hips bumped each other, as if she were simply his younger, teasing sister. I relaxed. That was it. Damon was always protective and was simply being a big brother to Katherine. And she needed that.

I whistled under my breath as I followed them. We had a small labyrinth in the front garden, but the maze on the far corner of the property was expansive, built from a boggy marsh by my father, who had been determined to impress our mother. She'd loved to garden and had always bemoaned the fact that the flowers that bloomed in her native France simply couldn't withstand the hard Virginia soil. The area always smelled of roses and clematis and was always the first place couples would retreat to when they wanted to be alone at a Veritas party. The servants had superstitions about the maze: that a child conceived in the maze would be blessed for life, that if you kissed your true love in the centre of the maze, you'd be bonded for life, but that if you told a lie while within its walls, you'd be cursed for ever. Today it felt almost magical: the arbours and vines provided shade from the sun, making it seem that the three of us were in an enchanted world together – away from death and war.

'It's even more beautiful than I remembered!'

Katherine explained. 'It's like a storybook. Like the Luxembourg Gardens or the Palace of Versailles!' She plucked a calla lily and inhaled deeply.

I paused and glanced at her. 'You've been to Europe, then?' I asked, feeling as provincial as any of the country bumpkins who lived in the shanty town on the other side of Mystic Falls, the ones who pronounced the word *creek* like *crick* and who already had four or five children by the time they were our age.

'I've been everywhere,' Katherine said simply. She tucked the lily behind her ear. 'So, tell me, boys, how did you amuse yourselves when you *didn't* have a mysterious stranger to impress with a tour of your grounds?'

'We entertain pretty young things with real Southern hospitality.' Damon smirked, falling into his overdone accent that always made me laugh.

Katherine rewarded him with a giggle, and I smiled. Now that I saw Damon and Katherine's flirtatious friendship as being as innocent as the relationship of cousins, I could enjoy their banter.

'Damon's right. Our Founders Ball is just a few weeks away.' I said, my spirits lifting as I realized that I was free to go to the ball with whoever I pleased. I couldn't wait to twirl Katherine in my arms.

'And you'll be the prettiest girl. Even the girls from Richmond and Charlottesville will be jealous!' Damon pronounced.

'Really? Why, I think I should like that. Is that

wicked of me?' Katherine asked, glancing from Damon to me.

'No,' I said.

'Yes,' Damon said at the same time. 'And I, for one, think more girls should admit their wicked natures. After all, we all know the fairer sex has a dark side. Remember when Clementine cut off Amelia's hair?' Damon turned to me.

'Yes,' I chuckled, happy to play the role of storyteller for Katherine's amusement. 'Clementine thought Amelia was being too forward with Matthew Hartnett, and since Clem wanted him, she decided she'd take it in her own hands to make Amelia less attractive.'

Katherine put her hand over her mouth in a gesture of exaggerated concern. 'I do hope poor Amelia's recovered.'

'She's engaged to some soldier. Don't worry about her,' Damon said. 'In fact, you shouldn't worry about anything. You're far too pretty.'

'Well, I am worried about one thing.' Katherine widened her eyes. 'Who shall escort me to the ball?' She swung her parasol back and forth on her arm as she gazed at the ground, as if thinking through a deep decision. My heart quickened as she looked up at both of us. 'I know! Let's have a race. Winner *may* get to take me!' She threw her parasol on the ground and ran off to the centre of the maze.

'Brother?' Damon asked, raising an eyebrow at me.

'Ready?' I smiled, as if this were just a casual children's footrace. I didn't want Damon to know how fast my heart was beating, and how very much I wanted to catch Katherine.

'Go!' Damon yelled. Immediately I began running. My hands and legs flailed, and I propelled myself into the maze. When we were in school, I was the fastest boy in the class, lightning quick when the school bell rang.

Then I heard peals of laughter. I glanced back. Damon was doubled up over himself, slapping his knee. I gulped air, trying not to seem winded. 'Scared to compete?' I said, running back and slugging him on the shoulder. I'd meant it to be a playful punch, but it landed with a heavy thud.

'Oh, now we're on, brother!' Damon said, his voice light and full of laughter. He grabbed my shoulders and wrestled me easily to the ground. I struggled to my feet and tackled him, throwing him onto his back and pinning down his wrists.

'Think you can still lick your little brother?' I teased, enjoying my momentary victory.

'No one came for me!' Katherine pouted, wandering out of the maze. Her frown quickly turned into a smile as she saw us on the ground, breathing heavily. 'Good thing I'm here to save you both.' She knelt and pressed her lips first to Damon's cheek, then to mine. I released Damon's wrists and stood up, wiping the dirt off my breeches.

'See?' she asked, as she offered an arm to Damon.

'All you need is a kiss to make everything better – although you boys shouldn't be such brutes with each other.'

'We were fighting for you,' Damon said lazily, not bothering to stand up. Just then, the sound of horses' hooves interrupted us. Alfred dismounted his horse and bowed to the three of us. It must have been a sight: Damon lying on the ground, resting his head on his hand as if he were simply reclining, me frantically brushing grass stains off my trousers, and Katherine standing between us, looking amused.

'I'm sorry to interrupt,' Alfred said. 'But Master Giuseppe needs to speak to Master Damon. It's urgent.'

'Of course it is. Everything is always urgent for Father. What do you bet he has another ridiculous theory he needs to discuss?' Damon said.

Katherine lifted her parasol from the ground. 'I should be going, too. I'm all dishevelled, and I'm due to visit with Pearl at the apothecary.'

'Come,' Alfred said, gesturing for Damon to jump onto the back of his horse. As Alfred and Damon rode away, Katherine and I slowly walked back to the carriage house. I wanted to bring up the Founders Ball again but found myself afraid to do so.

'You don't need to keep pace with me. Perhaps you should keep your brother company,' Katherine suggested. 'It seems that your father is a man who's best taken on by two,' she observed. Her hand brushed my own and she grabbed my wrist. Then she stepped on her tiptoes and allowed her lips to graze my cheek. 'Come see me tonight, sweet Stefan. My chambers will be open.' And with that, she broke off into a spirited run.

She was like a colt, galloping free, and I felt my heart gallop along with her. There was no question: she felt the same way I did. And knowing that made me feel more alive than I ever had in my life.

CHAPTER

15

As soon as twilight fell, I sneaked down the stairs, opened the back door, and tiptoed out onto the grass, already wet with dew. I was extra cautious, since there were torches surrounding the estate and I knew Father would be displeased that I was venturing out after dark. But the carriage house was only a stone's throw from the house itself – about twenty paces from the porch.

I stole across the yard, staying in the shadows, feeling my heart pound against my rib cage. I wasn't concerned about animal attacks or creatures of the night. I was more concerned that I'd be found by Alfred or, worse, Father. But the notion of not being able to see Katherine that night made me feel hysterical.

Once again, a heavy fog blanketed the ground and

rose to the sky, an odd reversal of nature that most likely was due to the changing of the seasons. I shivered and made sure to look away from the willow tree as I ran to the bridle path and up the porch steps of the carriage house.

I paused at the whitewashed door. The curtains on the windowpanes were pulled shut, and I couldn't see any candlelight seeping under the windows. For a second, I feared I had come too late. What if Katherine and Emily had retired to bed? Still, I rapped my knuckles sharply against the wooden door frame.

The door creaked open and a hand grabbed my wrist.

'Come in!' I heard a rough whisper as I was swept into the house. Behind me, I heard the click of the lock and realized I was standing face-to-face with Emily.

'Sir,' she said, smiling as she curtseyed. She was dressed in a simple navy gown, and her hair fell in dark waves around her shoulders.

'Good evening,' I said, bowing gently. I glanced around the little house, allowing my eyes to adjust to the dim light. A red lantern glowed on the rough-hewn table in the living room, casting shadows against the wooden beams of the ceiling. The carriage house had been in a state of disrepair for years, ever since Mother had died and her relatives had stopped visiting. But now that it was inhabited, there was a warmth to the rooms that was absent in the main house.

'What can I do for you, sir?' Emily asked, her dark eyes unblinking.

'Um . . . I'm here to see Katherine,' I stammered, suddenly embarrassed. What would Emily think of her mistress? Of course, maids are meant to be discreet, but I knew how servants talked, and I certainly didn't want Katherine's virtue to be compromised if Emily was the type to engage in idle servant gossip.

'Katherine has been expecting you,' Emily said, a glint of mischief in her dark eyes.

She took the lantern from the table and led me up the wooden stairs, stopping at the white door at the end of the hallway. I squinted. When Damon and I were little, we'd always been vaguely afraid of the upstairs of the carriage house. Maybe it was because the servants had said it was haunted, maybe because every floorboard had creaked, but something about the space had stopped us from staying very long. Now that Katherine was here, though, there was nowhere else I'd rather be.

Emily turned towards me, her knuckles on the door. She rapped three times. Then she swung the door open.

I walked cautiously into the room, the floorboards creaking as Emily disappeared down the hallway. The room itself was furnished simply: a cast-iron bed covered by a simple green quilt, an armoire in one corner, a washbasin in another, and a gilt-plated, freestanding mirror in a third corner.

Katherine sat on her bed, facing the window, her back to me. Her legs were tucked under her short white nightgown and her long curls were loose over her shoulders.

I stood there, watching her, then finally coughed.

She turned around, an expression of amusement in her dark, cat-like eyes.

'I'm here,' I said, shifting from one booted foot to the other.

'So I see.' she grinned. 'I watched you walk here. Were you frightened to be out after dark?'

'No!' I said defensively, embarrassed she'd seen me dart from tree to tree like an overcautious squirrel.

Katherine arched a dark eyebrow and held her arms out towards me. 'You need to stop worrying. Come here. I'll help you take your mind off things,' she said. I walked over to her as if in a dream, knelt on the bed, and hugged her tightly. As soon as I felt her body in my hands, I relaxed. Just feeling her was a reminder that she was real, that tonight was real, that nothing else mattered – not Father, not Rosalyn, not the spirits the townspeople were convinced roamed outside in the dark.

All that mattered was that my arms were around my love. Her hand worked its way down my shoulders, and I imagined us walking into the Founders Ball together. As her hand stopped at my shoulder blade and I felt her fingernails dig through the thin cotton of my shirt, I had a split-second image of us, ten years from now, with plenty of children who'd fill the estate with sounds of laughter. I wanted this life to be mine, now and forever. I moaned with desire and leaned in, allowing my lips to brush hers, first slowly, as we'd do in front of everyone when we announced our love at our wedding, and then harder and more urgently, allowing my lips to travel from her mouth to her neck, inching towards her snow-white bosom.

She grabbed my chin and pulled my face to hers and kissed me hard. I reciprocated. It was as if I were a starving man who'd finally found sustenance in her mouth. We kissed, and I closed my eyes and forgot about the future.

All of a sudden, I felt a sharp pain on my neck, as if I were being stabbed. I called out, but Katherine was still kissing me. But no, not kissing, *biting*, sucking the blood from beneath my skin. My eyes flew open, and I saw her eyes, wild and bloodshot, her face ghostly white in the moonlight. I wrenched my head back, but the pain was unrelenting, and I couldn't scream, couldn't fight, could only see the full moon out of the window, and could only feel the blood leaving my body, and desire and heat and anger and terror all welling up inside me. If this was what death felt like, then I wanted it. I wanted it, and that was when I flung my arms around Katherine, giving myself to her. Then everything faded to black.

CHAPTER
16

It was the lone hoot of an owl – a long, plaintive sound – that caused my eyes to snap open. As my eyes adjusted to the dim light, I felt a pulsing pain on the side of my neck that seemed to keep time with the owl's cries. And suddenly I remembered everything – Katherine, her lips drawn back, her teeth sparkling. My heart pounding as though I were dying and being born all at the same time. The awful pain, the red eyes, the dark black of a dead sleep. I glanced around wildly.

Katherine, clad only in a necklace and a simple muslin slip, sat just steps away from me at the basin, washing her upper arms with a hand towel. 'Hello, sleepy Stefan,' she said conquettishly.

I swung my legs out of bed and tried to step out, only to find myself tangled in the sheets. 'Your face,'

I babbled, knowing I sounded insane and possessed, like a town drunk stumbling out of the tavern.

Katherine continued to run the cotton cloth along her arms. The face I'd seen last night was not human. It had been a face filled with thirst and desire and emotions I couldn't even think to name. But in this light she looked lovelier than ever, blinking her eyes sleepily like a kitten after a long nap.

'Katherine?' I asked, forcing myself to look into her eyes. 'What are you?'

She slowly picked up the hairbrush on her nightstand, as if she had all the time in the world. She turned to me and began to run it through her luxuriant locks.

'You're not afraid, are you?' she asked.

So she *was* a vampire. My blood turned to ice.

I took the sheet and wrapped it around my body, then grabbed my breeches from the side of the bed and pulled them on. I quickly shoved my feet into my boots and yanked on my shirt, not caring about my undershirt, still on the floor. Fast as lightning, Katherine was at my side, her hand gripping my shoulder.

She was surprisingly strong, and I had to jerk sharply to wrench myself away from her grasp. Once free, she stepped back.

'Shhh. Shhh,' she murmured, as if she were a mother soothing a child.

'No!' I yelled, holding my hand up. I would *not* have her try to charm me. 'You're a vampire. You killed Rosalyn. You're killing the town. You are evil, and you need to be stopped.'

But then I caught sight of her eyes, her large, luminous, seemingly depthless eyes, and I stopped short.

'You're not afraid,' Katherine repeated.

The words echoed in my mind, bouncing around and finally taking residence there. I did not know how or why it was so, but in my heart of hearts, I suddenly wasn't afraid. But still . . .

'You are a vampire, though. How can I abide that?'

'Stefan. Sweet, scared Stefan. It will all work out. You'll see.' She cupped her chin in my hands, then raised up on her tiptoes for a kiss. In the near sunlight, her teeth looked pearly white and tiny, and nothing like the miniature daggers I'd seen the night before. 'It's me. I'm still Katherine,' she said, smiling.

I forced myself to pull away. I wanted to believe that everything was the same, but . . .

'You're thinking of Rosalyn, aren't you?' Katherine asked. She noticed my startled expression and shook her head. 'It's natural that you'd think I could do that, based on what I am, but I promise you, I did not kill her. And I never would have.'

'But . . . but . . .' I began.

She brought her finger to my lips. 'Shhh. I was with you that night. Remember? I care about you, and I care about those you care about. And I don't know how Rosalyn died, but whoever did that' – a flash of anger flickered in her eyes, which, I realized for the first time, were flecked with gold – 'they give us a bad name. They are the ones who scare me. You may be scared to walk during the night, but I am afraid to walk during the day, lest I be mistaken for one of those monsters. I may be a vampire, but I do have a heart. Please believe me, sweet Stefan.'

I took a step back and cradled my head in my hands. My mind whirled. The sun was just beginning to rise, and it was impossible to tell whether the mist hid a brilliant sun or a day of clouds. It was the same with Katherine. Her beautiful exterior cloaked her true spirit, making it impossible to ascertain whether she was good or evil. I sunk heavily to the bed, not wanting to leave and not wanting to stay.

'You need to trust me,' she said, sitting down beside me and placing her hand on my chest so she could feel my heart beat. 'I am Katherine Pierce. Nothing more, nothing less. I'm the girl you watched for hours on end after I arrived two weeks ago. What I confessed to you is *nothing*. It doesn't change how you feel, how I feel, what we can be,' she said, moving her hand from my chest to my chin. 'Right?' she asked, her voice filled with urgency.

I glanced at her wide brown eyes and knew she was right. She had to be.

My heart still desired her so much, and I wanted to do anything to protect her. Because she wasn't a *vampire*; she was Katherine. I grabbed both of her hands, cupping them in my own. They looked so small and vulnerable. I brought her cold, delicate fingers to my mouth and kissed them, one by one. She looked so scared and unsure.

'You didn't kill Rosalyn?' I said slowly. Even as the sentence left my lips, I knew it to be true, because my heart would break if it weren't.

Katherine shook her head and gazed at the window. 'I would never kill anyone unless I had to. Unless I needed to protect myself or someone I loved. And *anyone* would kill in that situation, wouldn't they?' she asked indignantly, jutting out her chin and looking so proud and vulnerable that it was all I could do not to take her in my arms right then. 'Promise you'll keep my secret, Stefan? Promise me?' she asked, her dark eyes searching mine.

'Of course I will,' I said, making the promise as much to myself as to her. I loved Katherine. And yes, she was a vampire. And yet . . . the way the word came out of her mouth was so different from the way it sounded when Father said it. There was no dread. If anything, it sounded romantic and mysterious. Maybe Father was wrong. Maybe Katherine was simply misunderstood.

'You have my secret, Stefan. And you know what that means?' she said, throwing her arms around my shoulders and nuzzling her cheek against mine. '*Vous avez mon coeur*. You have my heart.'

'And you have mine,' I murmured back, meaning every word.

CHAPTER

17

September 8, 1864
She is not who she seems. Should I be surprised?
Terrified? Hurt?

It's as if everything I know, everything I've been
taught, everything I've believed in my past seventeen
years is wrong.

I can still feel where she kissed me, where her
fingers grasped my hands. I still yearn for her, and yet
the voice of reason is screaming in my ears: you cannot
love a vampire!

If I had one of her daisies, I could pluck the petals
and let the flower choose for me. I love her . . . I love
her not . . . I . . .

I love her.

I do. No matter the consequences.

Is this what following your heart is? I wish there

was a map or a compass to help me find my way. But she has my heart, and that above all else is my North Star . . . and that will have to be enough.

After I slipped away from the carriage house back to my own chambers, I somehow managed to sleep for a few hours. When I awoke, I wondered if everything was all a dream. But then I shifted my head on the pillow and saw a neat puddle of dried, crimson blood and touched my fingers to my throat. I felt a wound there, and though it didn't hurt, it brought back the very real incidents of the previous evening.

I felt exhausted and confused and exalted all at once. My limbs were enervated, my brain abuzz. It was as if I had a fever, but inside I felt a sort of calm I'd never felt before.

I dressed for the day, taking extra care to wash the wound with a damp cloth and bandage it, then buttoned my linen shirt as high as it would go. I glanced at my reflection in the mirror. I tried to see if there was anything different, if there was some glint in my eye that acknowledged my newfound worldliness. But my face looked just as it had yesterday.

I crept down the back stairs towards the study. Father's schedule was like clockwork, and he always spent the mornings surveying and visiting the fields with Robert.

Once I closed myself in the cool, dark room, I ran my fingers along the leather-bound spines on each shelf, feeling comforted by their smoothness. I just hoped that somewhere, in the stacks and shelves of books on every subject, there would be a volume that would answer some of my questions. I remembered Katherine reading *The Mysteries of Mystic Falls* and noticed the volume was no longer in the study, or at least not in plain view.

I walked aimlessly from shelf to shelf, for the first time feeling overwhelmed by the number of books in Father's study. Where could I possibly find information on vampires? Father had volumes of plays, fiction, atlases and two full shelves of Bibles, some in English, some in Italian and some in Latin. I traced my hands against the gilt-lettered, leather spines of each book, hoping that somehow I'd find *something*.

Finally, my fingertips landed on a thin, tattered volume with *Demonios* written in flaking silver on the spine. *Demonio* . . . demon . . . This was what I was looking for. I opened the book, but it was written in an ancient Italian dialect that I couldn't make head nor tail of, despite my extensive tutoring in Latin and Italian.

Still, I carried the book with me to the club chair and settled in. Trying to decipher the book was an action I could understand, something easier than trying to eat breakfast while pretending everything was normal. I ran my fingers along the words, reading out loud as if I were a schoolboy, making sure I didn't miss a mention of the word *vampiro*. Finally,

I found it, but the sentences surrounding it were nothing but gibberish to me. I sighed in frustration.

Just then, the door to the study creaked open.

'Who's there?' I called loudly.

'Stefan!' My father's ruddy face registered surprise. 'I was looking for you.'

'Oh?' I asked, my hand flying to my neck, as if Father could see the bandage beneath the fabric. But all I felt was the smooth linen of my shirt. My secret was safe.

Father looked at me strangely. He walked towards me, taking the book off my lap. 'You and I think alike,' he said, a strange smile curving onto his face.

'We do?' My heart fluttered in my chest like a hummingbird's wings, and I was sure Father could hear my breath catching in short, shallow gasps in my throat. I felt sure he could read my thoughts, sure he *knew* about Katherine and me. And if he knew about Katherine, he'd kill her and . . .

I couldn't bear to think of the rest.

Father smiled again. 'We do. I know you took our conversation about vampires to heart, and I appreciate you taking this scourge seriously. Of course, I know you have your own motivations in avenging the death of your young Rosalyn,' Father said, making the sign of the cross over his chest.

I stared at a thin spot on the Oriental rug where the fabric was so faded that I could see the stained wooden floor below. I couldn't look up at Father and let my face betray my secret, betray Katherine's secret.

'Be assured, son, that Rosalyn did not die in vain. She died for Mystic Falls, and she will be remembered as we rid our town of this curse. And you, of course, will be an integral part of the plan.' Father gestured towards the book I still held. 'Unlike your good-for-nothing brother. What good is all his new military knowledge if he can't put it to use to defend his family, his land?' Father asked rhetorically. 'Just today he went off on a ride with some of his soldier friends. Even after I *told* him I expected him here this morning to accompany us to our meeting at Jonathan's house.'

But I wasn't paying attention anymore. All I cared about was that he didn't know about Katherine. My breathing slowed. 'There wasn't very much information that I could understand in this book. I don't think it's very useful,' I said, as if all I'd been doing this morning was indulging in a scholarly interest in vampires.

'That's just as well,' Father said dismissively, as he carelessly placed the book back on the shelf. 'I feel that together we have a good store of knowledge.'

'Together?' I parroted.

Father waved his hand impatiently. 'You and I and the Founders. We've set up a council to deal with this. We're heading to a meeting right now. You're coming.'

'I am?' I asked.

He glanced at me in annoyance. I knew I sounded like a simpleton, but there was too much information swimming in my mind to even begin to understand it all.

'Yes. And I'm taking Cordelia as well. She has a good knowledge of herbs and demons. The meeting is at Jonathan Gilbert's house.' Father nodded, as if the subject was closed.

I nodded as well, even though I was surprised. Jonathan Gilbert was a university teacher and sometimes inventor who Father not so privately called a crackpot. But now Father said his name with reverence. For the thousandth time that day, I realized this truly was a different world.

'Alfred is hitching up the carriage, but I will drive it. Do not tell *anyone* where we're going. I've already sworn Cordelia to secrecy,' Father said as he strode out of the room. After a second, I followed him, but not before I slipped *Demonios* into my back pocket.

I sat next to Father in the front seat of the carriage, while Cordelia sat in the back, hidden from sight lest she arouse suspicion. It was strange to be out in the morning, especially without a footman to drive us, and I caught the curious stares of Mr Vickery as we passed by the Blue Ridge Estate next door. I waved, until I felt Father's hand on my arm, a subtle warning not to attract attention to ourselves.

Father began talking once we entered the barren stretch of dirt road that separated the plantation from town. 'I don't understand your brother. Do you?

What man doesn't respect his father? If I didn't know better, I'd think he was consorting with one of *them*,' he said, spitting on the dirt road.

'Why would you think that?' I asked uncomfortably, a trickle of sweat running down my spine. I ran my finger beneath my collar, recoiling when I felt the gauze bandage on my neck. It was damp, but whether from sweat or blood I could not tell.

My thoughts were a tangle. Was I betraying Katherine by attending this meeting? Was I betraying Father by keeping Katherine's secret? Who *was* evil or good? Nothing seemed clear.

'I think that because *they* have that kind of power,' Father said, using the whip on Blaze as if to prove the point. Blaze whinnied before shifting into a fast trot.

I looked back at Cordelia, but she was impassively staring straight ahead.

'They can take over a mind before a man realizes anything is amiss. They compel them to submit fully to their charms and whims. Just a glance can make a man do whatever a vampire desires. And by the time a man *does* know he's being controlled, it's too late.'

'Really?' I asked skeptically. I thought back to last night. Had Katherine done that to me? But no. Even when I was frightened, I'd been myself. And all my feelings had been *mine*. Maybe vampires could do that, but Katherine certainly hadn't done it to me.

Father chuckled. 'Well, not all the time. One hopes that a man is strong enough to withstand that type of influence. And I certainly have raised my sons to be strong. Still, I wonder what could possibly have gotten into Damon's head.'

'I'm sure he's fine,' I said, suddenly very nervous at the idea that Damon might have figured out Katherine's secret. 'I think he's simply not sure what he wants.'

'I don't care what he wants,' Father said. 'What he needs to remember is that he's my son and I will not be disobeyed. These are dangerous times, much more so than Damon realizes. And he needs to understand that if he is not with us, people might construe that his sympathies lie elsewhere.'

'I think he just doesn't believe in vampires,' I said, a sick feeling forming in the pit of my stomach.

'Shhh!' Father whispered, waving his hand towards me to silence me. The horses were clip-clopping into town, just past the saloon, where Jeremiah Black was already nearly passed out by the door, a half bottle of whiskey at his feet.

Somehow, I didn't think Jeremiah Black was listening or even seeing what was going on, but I nodded, pleased that the silence gave me a chance to sort through my thoughts.

I glanced over to my right, where Pearl and her daughter were sitting on the iron bench outside the apothecary, fanning themselves. I waved to them, but, seeing Father's warning glance, thought better about calling out to say hello.

I closed my mouth and sat silently until we

reached the other end of town, where Jonathan Gilbert lived in an ill-kept mansion that had once belonged to his father. Father often made fun of the fact that the house was falling apart, but today he said nothing as he opened the door of the carriage.

'Cordelia,' Father called tersely, allowing her to walk up the rickety steps of the Gilbert mansion first as we followed suit.

Before we could ring the bell, Jonathan himself opened the door. 'Good to see you, Giuseppe, Stefan. And you must be Cordelia. I've heard much about your knowledge of native herbs,' he said, offering his hand to her.

Jonathan led us through the labyrinthine hallways and towards a tiny door next to the grand staircase. Jonathan opened it and gestured for us to head inside. We took turns ducking down to enter a tunnel that was about ten feet long, with a filmsy ladder at the other end. Wordlessly we climbed the ladder and emerged into a tiny, windowless space that immediately made me feel claustrophobic. Two candles burned in tarnished candleholders on a water-stained table, and as my eyes adjusted to the dim light, I could make out Honoria Fells sitting gingerly on a rocker in the corner. Mayor Lockwood and Sheriff Forbes shared an old wooden bench.

'Gentlemen,' Honoria said, standing up and welcoming us as if we were just stopping by for tea. 'And I'm afraid I haven't made your acquaintance, Mrs . . .' Honoria glanced suspiciously at Cordelia.

'Cordelia,' Cordelia murmured, glancing from one face to another, as if this was the last place she wanted to be.

My father coughed uncomfortably. 'She treated Stefan during his spells after his . . .'

'After his fiancée got her throat ripped out?' Mayor Lockwood said gruffly.

'Mayor!' Honoria said, clapping her hand to her mouth.

As Jonathan ducked back out into the hall, I settled on a straight-backed chair as far away from the group as possible. I felt out of place, though probably not as out of place as Cordelia, who was now awkwardly sitting on a wooden chair next to Honoria's rocker.

'Now, then!' Jonathan Gilbert said, coming back to the room, his arms laden with tools and papers and objects I couldn't even begin to identify. He sat on a moth-eaten velvet armchair at the head of the table and looked around. 'Let's begin.'

'Fire,' Father said simply.

A shiver of fear ran up my spine. Fire was how Katherine's parents had perished. Was that because they were vampires, too? Had Katherine been the only one to escape?

'Fire?' Mayor Lockwood repeated.

'It's been recorded, many times in Italy, that fire kills them, as does beheading or a stake in the heart. And, of course, there are herbs that can protect us.' Father nodded to Cordelia.

'Vervain,' Cordelia confirmed.

'Vervain,' Honoria said dreamily. 'How pretty.'

Cordelia snorted. 'It ain't nothing but a herb. But if you wear it, then you have protection from the devil. Some say it can also work a bit to nurse those who've been around them back to health. But it's poison to them devils you call vampires.'

'I want some!' Honoria said greedily, holding out her hand eagerly.

'I don't have any with me,' Cordelia said.

'You don't?' Father looked at her sharply.

'It's all gone from the garden. I used it for Mr Stefan's remedies; then when I went to pick it this morning, it was all gone. Was probably the children who took it,' Cordelia said indignantly, but she glanced straight at me. I looked away, reassuring myself that if she had known about Katherine's true nature, she would have told my father by now.

'Well, then, where do I get some?' Honoria asked.

'It's probably right under your nose,' Cordelia said.

'What?' asked Honoria sharply, as if she'd been insulted.

'It grows everywhere. Except our garden,' Cordelia said darkly.

'Well,' Father said, glancing at the two women, anxious to diffuse the situation. 'After this meeting, Cordelia may escort Miss Honoria to her garden to find vervain.'

'Now, wait just a damn minute,' Mayor Lockwood said, pounding his beefy fist on the table. 'You lost me at the woman talk. You mean to tell me that if I wear a lilac sprig, then the demons will leave me alone?' He snorted.

'Vervain, not lilac,' Cordelia explained. 'It keeps evil away.'

'Yes,' Father said sagely. 'And everyone in town must wear it. See to it, Mayor Lockwood. That way, not only will our citizens be protected, but anyone who does *not* wear it will be exposed as a vampire and can then be burned,' Father said, his voice so smooth and matter-of-fact that it took every ounce of self-control for me not to stand up, rush down the shaky ladder, find Katherine, and run away with her.

But if I did that, and if Katherine was as dangerous as the Founders thought . . . I felt like a trapped animal, unable to find any escape. Was I trapped with the enemy right now, or was the enemy back at Veritas? I knew that, beneath my shirt collar, the wound on my neck was beginning to ooze specks of blood, and it would only be a matter of time before they soaked through the fabric and stood out as a visible reminder of my betrayal.

Mayor Lockwood shifted uneasily, causing the chair to creak. I jumped. 'Now, if the herb works, that's one thing. But we're in the middle of a war. We've got a lot of Confederate government officials passing through Mystic Falls on their way to Richmond, and if word gets out that instead of aiding the cause we're fighting storybook creatures with flowers . . .' He shook his head. 'We cannot issue an edict that everyone wear vervain.'

'Oh, really? Then how do we know *you're* not a vampire?' Father demanded.

'Father!' I interjected. Someone had to bring a voice of reason into the discussion. 'Mayor Lockwood is right. We need to think calmly. Rationally.'

'Your son has a good head on his shoulders,' Mayor Lockwood said grudgingly.

'A better head than yours,' Father mumbled.

'Well . . . we can discuss vervain later. Honoria, you'll be in charge of making sure that we have a ready supply, and we can strongly encourage those we love to wear it. But for now, I want to discuss *other* ways we can find the vampires that walk among us,' Jonathan Gilbert said excitedly, unfolding large sheets of paper onto the table. Mayor Lockwood put his bifocals on his nose and peered at the papers, which had complicated mechanical drawings on them.

'This here looks like a compass,' Mayor Lockwood said finally, pointing to a complicated drawing.

'It is! But instead of finding north, it finds vampires,' Jonathan said, barely containing his excitement. 'I'm working on the prototype. It just needs a bit more fine-tuning. It's able to detect blood. The blood of others,' he said meaningfully.

'Can I see that, Mr Jonathan?' Cordelia asked.

Jonathan looked up, surprised, but handed her the papers. She shook her head.

'No,' she said. 'The prototype.'

'Oh, ah, well, it's *very rough*,' Jonathan said as he fumbled in his back pocket and pulled out a shiny metal object that looked more like a child's trinket than a tool for finding vampires.

Cordelia turned the compass slowly in her hands. 'It works?'

'Well . . .' – Jonathan shrugged – 'it *will* work.'

'Here's what I propose,' Father said, leaning back on his chair. 'We arm ourselves with vervain. We work day and night to get the compass to work. And we make a plan. We set up a siege, and by month's end our town will be clear.' Father crossed his arms in satisfaction. One by one, every member of the group, including Cordelia, nodded their heads.

I shifted on the wooden chair, holding my hand against my neck. The attic was hot and sticky, and flies were buzzing in the rafters, as if it were the middle of July rather than early September. I desperately needed a glass of water, and I felt like the room was going to collapse in on me. I needed to see Katherine again, to remind myself that she *wasn't* a monster. My breathing became shallow, and I felt that if I stayed here, I *would* say something I didn't mean.

'I think I'm feeling faint,' I heard myself say, even though the words rang false even to my ears. Father looked at me sharply. I could tell he didn't believe me, but Honoria clucked out sympathetic noises.

Father cleared his throat. 'I'll see my boy out,' he announced to the room before following me down the rickety ladder.

'Stefan,' he said, grabbing my shoulder just as I opened the door that would lead back to a world I understood.

'What?' I gasped.

'Remember. Not a word of this to anyone. Even Damon. Not until he comes to his senses. Except I think his senses may be taken with our Katherine,' Father muttered, half to himself as he let go of my arm. I stiffened at the mention of Katherine's name, but when I turned around, Father's back was towards me as he headed into the house.

I walked back through town, wishing I'd ridden Mezzanotte instead of coming in the carriage. Now I had no choice but to walk home. I turned to my left, deciding to cut through the forest. I simply couldn't interact with any more humans today.

CHAPTER

18

That night, Damon invited me to play cards with some of his soldier friends, who were camped out for the moment in Leestown, twenty miles away.

'I may not agree with them, but damn, can they play a good hand and drink a good pint,' Damon said.

I'd found myself agreeing, eager to avoid Father and any questions about vampires. But by the time twilight rolled around and I hadn't seen any sign of Katherine or Emily, I wished that I hadn't agreed to accompany Damon. My mind was still jumbled, and I wanted a night with Katherine to reassure me that my desire was leading me in the right direction. I loved her, but the practical, sensible side of me was having trouble disobeying Father.

'Ready?' Damon asked, clad in his Confederate uniform, when he stopped by my bedroom at twilight.

I nodded. It was too late to say no.

'Good.' He grinned and clattered down the stairs. I glanced wistfully out of the window at the carriage house, then followed him.

'We're going out to the camp,' Damon yelled as we passed by Father's study.

'Wait!' Father emerged from the study into the living room, several long branches filled with tiny, lilac-like purple flowers in his arms. Vervain. 'Wear this,' he commanded, tucking a sprig into each of our breast pockets.

'You shouldn't have, Father,' Damon said tersely, as he plucked the sprig out of his pocket and shoved it into his breeches pocket.

'I've given you latitude, son, and given you a roof. Now all I ask is that you do this,' Father said, slamming his meaty fist into his palm so hard, I saw him wince. Thankfully, Damon, usually so quick to pounce at any sign of weakness, didn't notice.

'Fine, Father.' Damon shrugged easily and spread his arms as if in defeat. 'I would be *honoured* to wear your flower for you.'

Father's eyes flickered with rage, but he didn't say anything. Instead, he simply broke off another sprig and tucked it into Damon's coat pocket.

'Thank you,' I mumbled as I accepted my own branch. My statement of thanks was less for the flower and more for Father showing mercy on Damon.

'Be careful, boys,' Father said, before retreating to his study.

Damon rolled his eyes as we walked outside.

'You shouldn't be so hard on him,' I mumbled, shivering in the night air. The summer-like day had become a chilly fall evening, but the mist that had been everywhere last night had lifted, giving us a crystal-clear view of the moon.

'Why not? He's hard on us.' Damon snorted as he led the way to the stable. Mezzanotte and Jake were already bridled and stamping their hooves impatiently. 'I had Alfred get everything ready. Thought we'd need a quick getaway.'

Damon swung his leg over Jake's back, then galloped him down the path and turned in the direction opposite to town. We rode in silence for at least a half hour. With just the sound of the hooves and the sight of the moon peeking through the dense foliage, it felt like we were riding into a dream.

Finally, we began to hear sounds of flutes playing and laughter and the occasional gunshot. Damon directed us up over a hill towards a clearing. Tents were set up all over, and a piper played in the corner. Men were walking around, and dogs were stationed at the entrance. It was as if we'd arrived at a mysterious hidden party.

'Hello, sir?' Two Confederate soldiers came up to us, their rifles pointed at us. Mezzanotte took a few steps back and whinnied nervously.

'Soldier Damon Salvatore, sir! Here on leave from

General Groom's camp down in Atlanta.'

Immediately, the two soldiers relaxed their rifles and tipped their hats at us.

'Sorry 'bout that, soldier. We're gearin' up for battle, and we're losing our men like flies, before they even hit the battlefield,' the taller soldier said, stepping up to pat Jake.

'Yes, and not because of typhus,' the other, smaller, mustachioed soldier said, obviously pleased to share this information with us.

'Killings?' Damon asked tersely.

'How'd you know?' the first guard asked, stroking his rifle. I glanced at the ground, unsure what to do. I felt that Damon was getting us into a dangerous situation, but I didn't know what I could do to fix it.

'My brother and I are coming from Mystic Falls,' Damon said, jerking his thumb back as if to prove that was the direction we came from. 'The next town over, past the forest. We've had some of our own trouble. People are saying it's some type of animal.'

'Not unless it's an animal that only goes for the throat and leaves the rest of the body untouched,' the mustachioed soldier said knowledgeably, his tiny eyes flicking back and forth between us.

'Hmm,' Damon said, sounding suddenly uninterested. But then he changed the subject. 'Any good games of poker going on tonight?'

'Right there in that clearing by the oak trees.' The

small soldier pointed a little way off into the distance.

'Have a good evening, then. I thank you for your help,' Damon said with exaggerated politeness. We walked the horses in the direction the soldier pointed, until Damon stopped abruptly at a small circle of soldiers, huddled around a fire and playing cards.

'Hello! Soldier Damon Salvatore on leave from General Groom's boys,' Damon said confidently as he slid off his horse and glanced around the faces lit up by the campfire. 'This is my brother, Stefan. Can we be dealt in?'

One ginger-haired soldier glanced at an older, grandfatherly type whose arm was in a sling. He shrugged and gestured for us to sit on one of the logs set up around the fire. 'Don't see why not.'

Adrenaline seeped through my veins as we settled down and took our hands. Mine was good: two aces and a king. I immediately threw in some rumpled notes from my pocket, making a bet with myself. If I won money, then everything would be fine with Katherine. And if I didn't, then . . . well, I didn't want to think about it.

'All in,' I said confidently.

After we settled the game, I wasn't surprised to emerge as the victor. I smiled as I took the pile of money and carefully put it in my pocket. I grinned in relief, finally feeling sure in my love for Katherine. I imagined what she would say. *Smart* Stefan, maybe. *Savvy* Stefan. Or maybe she'd simply laugh, showing her white teeth, and allow me to take her into my arms and twirl her around and around the room. . . .

We played several more hands after that, during which I lost the money I had won, but I didn't care. The first hand had been the test, and now my heart and mind felt remarkably light.

'What are you thinking?' Damon asked, taking a flask from his pocket. He held it towards me, and I took a long swig.

The whiskey burned going down my throat, but I still craved more. It didn't seem that any of the other soldiers were up for another hand. The five we were playing with had drifted off to chew tobacco, drink more whiskey, or tearfully talk about their sweethearts back home.

'Come on, brother, you can tell me,' Damon encouraged. He took the flask, swigged from it, then passed it back to me.

I took another, deeper drink and paused. Should I tell him? Any hesitation I had earlier had disappeared. After all, he was *my brother*. 'Well, I was thinking about how different Katherine is than any other girl I've met . . .' I began evasively. I knew I was treading into dangerous territory, but part of me was dying to know whether Damon also knew Katherine's secret. I took another sip of whiskey and coughed.

'How's she different?' Damon asked, a smile curving on his lips.

'Well, I mean she's not,' I said, sobering up as I

frantically tried to backtrack. 'I just meant that I noticed that she is—'

'That she's a vampire?' he interrupted.

My breath caught in my throat, and I blinked. I glanced around nervously. People were drinking, laughing, counting their winnings.

But Damon was simply sitting there, the same smile on his lips. I couldn't understand how he was *smiling*. And then a new, darker thought appeared in my mind. How did Damon know that Katherine was who she was? Had she told him? And had it been the same way, in the misty predawn, in bed? I shuddered.

'So she's a vampire. What of it? She's still Katherine.' He turned to look at me, urgency in his dark-brown eyes. 'And you won't say anything to Father. He's half crazy as it is,' he said as he scuffed his boot against the ground.

'How did you find out?' I couldn't stop myself from asking.

Suddenly, a shot was fired.

'Soldier down!' a uniformed boy who looked to be about fourteen yelled as he charged from tent to tent. 'Soldier down! Attack! Out into the woods!'

Damon's face paled. 'I need to help. You, little brother, go home.'

'Are you sure?' I asked, feeling torn and suddenly frightened.

He nodded tersely. 'If Father asks, I drank too much at the saloon and am sleeping it off somewhere.'

Another shot was fired, and Damon took off into the woods, blending into the sea of soldiers.

'Go!' he yelled. I ran in the opposite direction to the now-abandoned camp and dug my heels into Mezzanotte, whispering in her velvety ears and imploring her to go faster.

Mezzanotte rode through the forest faster than she ever had before; once across the Wickery Bridge, she turned, as if she knew exactly how to head home. But then she reared and whinnied. I held on with my thighs and saw a shadowy figure with golden-brown hair, arm-in-arm with another girl.

I stiffened. No women would be out after dark unaccompanied by a man in the best of circumstances, but *definitely* not in these times. Not with the vampire attacks.

The face turned, and in the reflection on the water I saw a pale, pointed face. *Katherine.* She was escorting little Anna from the apothecary. All I could see were the dark vines of Anna's curls, bouncing over her shoulders.

'Katherine!' I yelled from the horse, with a strength I did not know I possessed. Now, instead of wanting to hold her, I wanted to use my arms to restrain her, to make her stop carrying out the awful thing she was about to do. I felt bile rise in my throat as I imagined finding a jagged branch and ramming it into her chest.

Katherine didn't turn around. She held Anna's shoulders tighter and led her into the forest. I kicked

Mezzanotte hard on the flanks, the wind whipping against my face as I desperately tried to catch up with them.

CHAPTER

19

I galloped through the woods, kicking Mezzanotte to jump over logs, to dash through underbrush, anything to make sure I didn't lose sight of Katherine and Anna. How *could* I have trusted Katherine? How could I have thought I *loved* her? I should have killed her when I had the chance. If I didn't catch up to them, Anna's blood would be on my hands, too. Just as Rosalyn's was.

We reached an uprooted tree and Mezzanotte reared up, sending me tumbling backwards onto the forest floor. I felt a sharp stab as my temple cracked against a stone. The wind was knocked out of me, and I fought for breath, knowing it was only a matter of time before Katherine would kill Anna and then finish me off.

I felt gentle, ice-cold hands lifting me up to a

sitting position.

'No . . .' I gasped. The act of breathing hurt. My breeches were ripped, and I had a large gash on my knee. Blood flowed freely from my temple.

Katherine knelt beside me, using the sleeve of her dress to stave off the bleeding. I noticed her licking her lips, then mashing them firmly together. 'You're hurt,' she said softly, continuing to apply pressure to my wound. I pushed myself away from her, but she clasped my shoulder, holding me in place.

'Don't worry. Remember. You have my heart,' Katherine said, holding my gaze with hers. Wordlessly, I nodded. If death was to come, I hoped it would come quickly. Sure enough, she bared her teeth, and I closed my eyes, waiting for the agonizing ecstasy of her teeth against my neck.

But nothing came. Instead, I felt her cold skin near my mouth.

'Drink,' Katherine commanded, and I saw a thin gash in her delicate white skin. Blood was trickling from the cut as though through a brook after a rainstorm. I was repulsed and tried to turn my head away, but Katherine held on to the back of my neck. 'Trust me. It will help.'

Slowly, fearfully, I allowed my lips to touch the liquid. Immediately I felt warmth run down my throat. I continued to drink until Katherine pulled her arm away.

'That's enough,' she murmured, holding her palm over the wound. 'Now, how do you feel?' She sat back on her heels and surveyed me.

How did I feel? I touched my leg, my temple. Everything felt smooth. Healed.

'You did that,' I said incredulously.

'I did.' Katherine stood up and brushed her hands together. I noticed her wound, too, was now completely healed. 'Now tell me why I had to heal you. What are you doing in the forest? You know it's not safe,' she said, concern belying her chiding tone.

'You . . . Anna,' I murmured, feeling sluggish and sleepy, as one might feel after a long, wine-infused dinner. I blinked at my surroundings. Mezzanotte was hitched to a tree, and Anna was sitting on a low branch, hugging her knees to her chest and watching us. Instead of terror, Anna's face was full of confusion as she looked from me, to Katherine, then back to me.

'Stefan, Anna is one of my friends,' Katherine said simply.

'Does Stefan . . . know?' Anna asked curiously, whispering as if I wasn't standing three feet from her.

'We can trust him,' Katherine said, nodding definitively.

I cleared my throat, and both girls looked at me.

'What are you doing?' I asked finally.

'Meeting,' Katherine said, gesturing to the clearing.

'Stefan Salvatore,' a throaty voice said. I whirled around and saw a third figure emerge from the shadows. Almost without thinking, I held up the vervain from my breast pocket, which looked as useless as a daisy clutched in my hand.

'Stefan Salvatore,' I heard again. I glanced wildly between Anna and Katherine, but their facial expressions were impossible to read. An owl hooted, and I pressed my fist into my mouth to keep from screaming.

'It's okay, Mama. He knows,' Anna called to the shadows.

Mama. So that meant Pearl was also a vampire. But how could she be? She was the apothecary, the one who was supposed to heal the sick, not tear out human throats with her teeth. Then again, Katherine had healed me, and she hadn't torn out my throat.

Pearl emerged from between the trees, her gaze tightening on me. 'How do we know he's safe?' she asked suspiciously, in a voice that was much more ominous than the polite tone she used at her apothecary.

'He is,' Katherine said, smiling sweetly as she gently touched my arm. I shivered and clutched the vervain, Cordelia's words echoing in my head. *This herb could stop the devil.* But what if we'd all gotten it wrong, and vampires like Katherine weren't devils but angels? What then?

'Drop the vervain,' Katherine said. I looked into her large, cat-like eyes and dropped the plant to the forest floor. Immediately, she used the tip of her boot to cover it with pine needles and leaves.

'Stefan, you look as though you've seen a ghost,'

Katherine laughed, turning towards me. But her laughter wasn't mean. Instead, it sounded melodic and musical and slightly sad. I collapsed onto a gnarled tree root. I noticed my leg was shaking and held my hands firmly against my knee, which was now completely smooth, as if the fall had never happened. She took the motion as an invitation for her to perch on my knee. She sat and looked down at me, running her hands through my hair.

'Now, Katherine, he doesn't look like he's seen a ghost. He's seen vampires. Three of them.' I glanced up at Pearl as if I were an obedient schoolboy and she were my schoolmarm. She sat down on a nearby rock slab, and Anna perched next to her, suddenly looking much younger than her fourteen years. But, of course, if Anna was a vampire, then that meant she wasn't fourteen at all. My brain spun, and I felt a momentary wave of dizziness. Katherine patted the back of my neck, and I began to breathe easier.

'Okay, Stefan,' Pearl said as she rested her chin on her steepled fingers and gazed at me. 'First of all, I need you to remember that Anna and I are your neighbours, and your friends. Can you remember that?'

I was transfixed by her gaze. Pearl then smiled a curious half smile. 'Good,' she exhaled.

I nodded dumbly, too overwhelmed to think, let alone speak.

'We were living in South Carolina right after the war,' Pearl began.

'*After* the war?' I asked, before I could stop myself.

Anna giggled, and Pearl cracked a tiny sliver of a smile. 'The War of Independence,' Pearl explained briefly. 'We were lucky during the war. All safe, all sound, all a family.' Her voice caught in her throat, and she closed her eyes for a moment before continuing. 'My husband ran a small apothecary when a wave of consumption hit town. Everyone was affected – my husband, my two sons, my baby daughter. Within a week, they were dead.'

I didn't know what to say. Could I say I was sorry for something that had happened so long ago?

'And then Anna began coughing. And I *knew* I couldn't lose her, too. My heart would break, but it was more than that,' Pearl said, shaking her head as if caught in her own world. 'I knew my *soul* and my *spirit* would break. And then I met Katherine.'

I glanced at Katherine. She looked so young, so innocent. I glanced away before she could look at me.

'Katherine was different,' Pearl said. 'She arrived in town mysteriously, without relatives, but she immediately became part of society.'

I nodded, wondering who, then, was killed in the Atlanta fire that brought Katherine to Mystic Falls. But I didn't ask, waiting for Pearl to continue her story.

She cleared her throat. 'Still, there was something about her that was unusual. All the ladies and I talked about it. She was beautiful, of course, but there was something else. Something otherworldly.

Some called her an angel. But then she never got sick, not during the cold seasons, and not when the consumption began in town. There were certain herbs she wouldn't touch in the apothecary. Charleston was a small town then. People talked.'

Pearl reached for her daughter's hand. 'Anna would have died,' Pearl continued. 'That's what the doctor said. I was desperate for a cure, wracked with grief and feeling so helpless. Here I was, a woman surrounded by medicine, unable to help my daughter live.' She shook her head in disgust.

'So what happened?' I asked.

'I asked Katherine one day if she knew of anything that could be done. And as soon as I asked, I *knew* she did. There was something in her eyes that changed. But she still took a few minutes of silence before she responded and then –'

'Pearl brought Anna to my chambers one night,' Katherine interjected.

'She saved me,' Anna said in a soft voice. 'Mother too.'

'And that's how we ended up here. We couldn't stay in Charleston forever, never growing old,' Pearl explained. 'Of course, soon we'll have to move again. That's the way it goes. We're gypsies, navigating between Richmond and Atlanta and all the towns in between. And now we have *another* war to deal with. Seeing so much history really proves to us that some things never do change,' Pearl said, smiling ruefully. 'But there are worse ways to pass the time.'

'I like it here,' Anna admitted. 'That's why I'm scared we'll be sent away.' She said that last part as a whisper, and something about her tone made me achingly sad.

I thought of the meeting I'd attended that afternoon. If Father had his way, they wouldn't be sent away, they'd be killed.

'The attacks?' I asked finally. It had been the one question that had been nagging at me ever since Katherine's confession. Because if she didn't do it, then who . . . ?

Pearl shook her head. 'Remember, we're your neighbours and friends. It wasn't us. We never would behave like that.'

'Never,' Anna parroted, shaking her head fearfully, as though she were being accused.

'But some of our tribe have,' Pearl said darkly.

Katherine's eyes hardened. 'But it's not just *we* or the other vampires who are causing trouble. Of course, that's who everyone blames, but no one seems to remember that there's a war going on with untold bloodshed. All people care about are vampires.' Hearing Damon's words in Katherine's mouth was like a bucket of cold water in my face, a reminder that I wasn't the only person in her universe.

'Who are the other vampires?' I asked gruffly.

'It's our community, and we will take care of it,' Pearl said firmly. She stood up, then walked across the clearing, her feet crunching on the ground until she stood above me. 'Stefan, I've told you the story and now here are the facts: we need blood to live. But we don't need it from humans,' Pearl said, as if she were explaining to one of her customers how a herb worked. 'We can get it from animals. But, like humans, some of us don't have self-control, and some of us attack people. It's really not that much different from a rogue soldier, is it?'

I suddenly had an image of one of the soldiers we'd just played poker with. Were any of them vampires, too?

'And remember, Stefan, we only know some. There could be more. We're not as uncommon as you may think,' Katherine said.

'And now, because of these vampires we don't even know, we're all being hunted,' Pearl said, tears filling her eyes. 'That's why we're meeting here tonight. We need to discuss what to do and come up with a plan. Just this afternoon, Honoria Fells brought a vervain concoction to the apothecary. How that woman even *knows* about vervain, I have no idea. Suddenly, I feel like I'm an animal about to be trapped. People have glanced at our necks, and I know they're wondering about our necklaces, piecing together the fact that all three of us always wear them . . .' Pearl trailed off as she raised her hands to the sky, as if in an exasperated prayer.

Quickly, I glanced at each of the women and realized that Anna and Pearl were wearing ornate cameos like the one Katherine wore.

'The necklace?' I asked, clutching my own throat as if I, too, had a mysterious blue gem there.

'Lapis lazuli. It allows us to walk in daylight. Those of our kind cannot, usually. But these gems protect us. They've allowed us to live normally and, perhaps, even allowed us to stay more in touch with our human side than we would have otherwise,' Pearl said thoughtfully. 'You don't know what it's like, Stefan.' Pearl's matter-of-fact voice dissolved into sobs. 'It's good to know that we have friends we can trust.'

I took out my handkerchief from my breast pocket and handed it to her, unsure what else I could do. She dabbed her eyes and shook her head. 'I'm sorry. I'm so sorry that you have to know about this, Stefan. I knew from the last time that war changes things, but I never thought . . . it's too soon to have to move again.'

'I'll protect you,' I heard myself saying, in a voice that didn't quite sound like mine.

'But . . . but . . . how?' Pearl asked. Far off in the distance a branch broke and all four of us jumped. Pearl glanced around. 'How?' she said again, finally, when all was still.

'My father's leading a charge in a few weeks.' I felt a tiny pinprick of betrayal as I said it.

'Giuseppe Salvatore.' Pearl gasped in disbelief. 'But how did he know?'

I shook my head. 'It's Father and Jonathan Gilbert and Honoria Fells and Mayor Lockwood and Sheriff

Forbes. They seem to know about vampires from books. Father has an old volume in his study, and together they came up with the idea to lead a siege.'

'Then he'll do it. Giuseppe Salvatore is not a man to have his opinions easily swayed,' Pearl stated.

'No, ma'am.' I realized how funny it was to call a vampire *ma'am*. But who was I to say what was normal and what wasn't? Once again, my mind drifted to my brother and his words, his casual laughter when it came to Katherine's true nature. Maybe it *wasn't* that Katherine was evil, or uncommon at all. Maybe the only thing that was uncommon was the fact that Father was fixated on eradicating the vampires.

'Stefan, I promise that nothing I've said to you was a lie,' Pearl said. 'And I know that we will do everything in our power to ensure that no more animals or humans are killed as long as we're here. But you simply *must* do what you can. For us. Because Anna and I have come too far and gone through too much to simply be killed by our neighbours.'

'You won't be,' I said, with more conviction than I ever had in my life. 'I'm not sure what I'll do yet, but I will protect you. I promise.' I was making the promise to the three of them, but was looking only at Katherine. She nodded, a tiny spark igniting in her eyes.

'Good,' Pearl said, reaching out her hand to help a sleepy-eyed Anna to her feet. 'Now, we've been here in the forest too long. The less we're seen together, the better. And, Stefan, we trust you,' she said, with just the tiniest hint of a warning in her otherwise rich voice.

'Of course,' I said, grabbing Katherine's hand as Anna and Pearl walked out of the clearing. I wasn't worried about them. Because they worked at the apothecary, they could get away with walking in the middle of the night; they could easily tell anyone who saw them that they were searching for herbs and mushrooms.

But I was scared for Katherine. Her hands felt so small, and her eyes looked so frightened. She was depending on me, a thought that filled me with equal amounts of pride and dread.

'Oh, Stefan,' she said as she flung her arms around my neck. 'I know everything will be fine as long as we're together.' She grabbed my hand and pulled me onto the forest floor. And then, lying with Katherine amid the pine needles and the damp earth and the smell of her skin, I wasn't frightened anymore.

CHAPTER

20

I didn't see Damon for the next few days. Father said he was spending time at the camp, an idea that clearly filled him with no small amount of pleasure. Father hoped that Damon spending time there would lead to him rejoining the army, even though I figured his hours would be spent mostly gambling and talking about women. I, for one, was glad. Of course, I missed my brother, but I would never be able to spend so much uninterrupted, unquestioned time with Katherine if Damon was around.

Truthfully, although I felt disloyal to say it, Father and I adapted well to Damon being gone. We began taking meals together, companionably playing hands of cribbage after dinner. Father would share his thoughts about the day, about the overseer and about his plans to buy new horses from a farm in Kentucky.

For the hundredth time, I realized how much he wanted me to take over the estate, and for the first time, I felt excitement in that possibility.

It was because of Katherine. I'd taken to spending each night in her chambers, leaving just before work began in the fields. She hadn't bared her fangs since that night in the woods. It was as if that secret meeting in the forest had changed everything. She needed me to keep her secret, and I needed her to keep me whole. In her small dim bedroom, everything was passionate and perfect – it almost felt as if we were newlyweds.

Of course, I wondered how it would work, me growing older each year as Katherine stayed just as young and beautiful. But that was a question for later, after the fear of the vampire scourge was over, after we were engaged, after we'd settled into a life without hiding.

'I know you've been spending time with young Katherine,' Father said one night at the dinner table, as Alfred cleared the table and brought Father his well-worn deck of cards for us to play.

'Yes.' I watched as Alfred poured port into Father's glass. In the flickering candlelight, the normally pink liquid looked like blood. He held the decanter to me, but I shook my head.

'So has young Damon,' Father observed, taking the card deck in his thick fingers and slowly palming it from hand to hand.

I sighed, annoyed that Damon had once again

come into a conversation about Katherine. 'She needs a friend. *Friends*,' I said.

'That she does. And I'm glad that you've been able to provide her with companionship,' Father said. He placed the cards facedown on the table and glanced at me.

'You know, I don't know very much about her Atlanta relations. I'd heard of her through one of my shipping partners. Very sad, a girl orphaned by Sherman's battle, but there aren't very many other Pierces that say they know of her.'

I shifted nervously. 'Pierce is a common enough name. And maybe she doesn't want to be affiliated with some of her relations.' I took a deep breath. 'I'm sure there are other Salvatores out there that we haven't heard of.'

'There's a good point,' Father said, taking a sip of his port. 'Salvatore *isn't* a common name, but it's a good one. Which is why I hope you and Damon know what you're getting into.'

I looked up sharply.

'Fighting over the same girl,' Father said simply. 'I wouldn't want you to lose your relationship. I know I don't always see eye to eye with your brother, but he's your flesh and blood.'

I cringed, the familiar phrase suddenly complicated. But if Father noticed, he didn't say anything. He picked up the deck and glanced at me expectantly. 'Shall we play?' he asked, already beginning to deal six cards to me.

I picked up my stack, but instead of looking at the cards, I glanced out of the corner of my eye, to see if I could spot any movement from the carriage house through the window.

Alfred walked into the room. 'Sir, you have a guest.'

'A guest?' Father asked curiously, half standing up from the table. We rarely had guests come to the estate unless there was a party. Father always preferred meeting acquaintances in town or at the tavern.

'Please forgive my intrusion.' Katherine walked in, her thin arms filled with a bouquet of flowers of all different shapes and sizes – roses and hydrangeas and lilies of the valley. 'Emily and I were picking the flowers by the pond, and I thought you might appreciate some colour.' Katherine offered a small grin as Father stiffly held out his hand for her to shake. He'd barely had a four-word conversation with her since she'd arrived. I held my breath, as anxious as I would be if I were introducing Father to my betrothed.

'Thank you, Miss Pierce,' Father said. 'And our house is your house. Please don't feel you need to ask permission to come visit. We'd love to have you, whenever you wish to spend time with us.'

'Thank you. I wouldn't want to be an imposition,' she said, batting her eyelashes in a way that was irresistible for any man.

'Please, have a seat,' Father said, settling back down at the head of the table. 'My son and I were just preparing to play a hand of cards, but we can certainly put them away.'

Katherine eyed our game. 'Cribbage! My father and I always used to play. May I join you?' She flashed a smile as she settled into my chair and picked up my hand. Instantly, she frowned and began rearranging the cards.

How could she, when worried for her very existence, be so carefree and enchanting?

'Why, of course, Miss Pierce. If you'd like to play, I'd be honoured, and I'm sure my son would be happy to help you.'

'Oh, I know how to play.' She set a card in the centre of the table.

'Good,' Father said, putting his own card on top of hers. 'And, you know, I do worry about you and your maid, all alone in the carriage house. If you want to move to the main house, please, just let me know and your wish is my command. I thought that you would like some privacy, but with things as they are and all the danger . . .' he trailed off.

Katherine shook her head, a shadow of a frown crossing her face. 'I'm not frightened. I lived through a lot in Atlanta,' she said, placing an ace on the table faceup. 'Besides, the servants' quarters are so close, they would hear me if I screamed.'

As Father placed a seven of spades on the table, Katherine touched my knee, slowly brushing it with a feathery stroke. I flushed at the intimate contact when my father was so close, but I didn't want her to stop.

She placed a five of diamonds on the card pile. 'Thirteen. I think I may be on a lucky streak, Mr Salvatore,' she said, moving her peg one spot on the cribbage board.

Father broke into a delighted grin. 'You're quite a girl. Stefan's never really understood the rules of this game.'

The door slammed, and Damon walked into the room, his rucksack over his shoulder. He shrugged it off onto the floor, and Alfred picked it up. Damon didn't seem to notice. 'Looks like I'm missing all the fun,' he said, his tone accusatory as his gaze flicked from Father back to me.

'You are,' Father said simply. Then he actually glanced up and smiled at him. 'Young Katherine here is proving that she's not only beautiful but that she has brains, too. An intoxicatingly infuriating combination,' Father said, noticing that she had racked up an additional point on the board when he wasn't looking.

'Thank you,' Katherine said, deftly discarding and picking up a new card. 'You're making me blush. Although I do admit that I think your compliments are just an elaborate plan for distracting me so you can win,' she said, barely bothering to acknowledge Damon.

I strode over to Damon. We stood together in the doorway, watching Katherine and Father.

Damon crossed his arms over his chest. 'What is she doing here?'

'Playing cards.' I shrugged.

'Do you really think that's wise?' Damon lowered his voice. 'Given his opinions on her . . . *provenance*.'

'But don't you see? It's brilliant. She's charming him. I haven't heard him laugh so hard since Mother died.' I felt suddenly delirious with happiness. *This* was better than anything I could have planned. Instead of trying to come up with an elaborate plot to push Father off the vampire trail, he would simply see that Katherine was *human*. That she still had emotions and wouldn't do any harm save for ruining his winning streak at cribbage.

'So what?' Damon asked. 'He's a madman on the hunt. A few smiles won't change that.'

Katherine erupted into giggles as Father put down a card. I lowered my voice. 'I think if we let him know about her, he'd change his mind. He'd realize that she doesn't mean any harm.'

'Are you crazy?' Damon hissed, clenching my arm. His breath smelled like whiskey. 'If Father knew about Katherine, he'd kill her in an instant! How do you know he's not already planning something?'

Just then Katherine let out a peal of laughter. Father threw his head back, adding his hoarse laugh to hers. Damon and I fell silent as she glanced up from her cards. She found us with her eyes and winked.

But since Damon and I were standing side by side, it was impossible to tell who it was meant for.

CHAPTER

21

The next morning, Damon left with the brief explanation that he was helping the militia at the camp. I wasn't sure I believed his excuse, but the house was decidedly more peaceful in his absence. Katherine came over each night to play cribbage with Father. Occasionally I'd join her as a two-against-one team.

While playing, she would tell Father stories from her past: about her father's shipping business; about her Italian mother; about Wheat, the Scottish terrier she'd had as a girl. I wondered if any of them were true, or if it was Katherine's plan to act as a modern-day Scheherazade, spinning stories that would eventually persuade Father to spare her.

Katherine would always make a show of going back to the carriage house, and it was agony waiting for the moment when Father went to bed so that I could follow her. She never talked about her past – or her plans – with me. She didn't tell me how she got her nourishment, and I didn't ask. I didn't want to know. It was far easier to pretend she was just a normal girl.

One afternoon, when Father was in town with Robert, discussing business with the Cartwrights, Katherine and I decided to spend an entire day together, instead of a few stolen, dark hours. It was nearing October, but no one would know it from the high temperatures and the daily late-afternoon thunderstorms. I hadn't gone swimming all summer, and I couldn't wait to feel the water of the pond on my skin – and Katherine in my arms in the daylight. I stripped down and jumped in immediately.

'Don't splash!' yelled Katherine. She lifted her simple blue skirt up to her ankles and cautiously stepped towards the edge of the pond. She'd already left her muslin flats beneath the willow tree, and I couldn't stop staring at the delicate white of her ankles.

'Come in! The water's fine!' I yelled, even though my teeth were chattering.

She continued to tiptoe towards the edge of the pond until she was standing on the muddy strip between the grass and the water. 'It's dirty.' She wrinkled her nose, shielding her eyes from the sun.

'That's why you have to get in. To wash off all the mud,' I said, using my fingers to flick water at her. A few droplets landed on the bodice of her dress, and I felt desire course through me. I dunked under the water to cool my head.

'You're not afraid of a little splashing,' I said as I emerged, my hair dripping on my shoulders. 'Or, shall I say, you're not afraid of splashing Stefan?' I felt a little bit ridiculous saying it, because such comments didn't sound nearly as clever on my lips. Still, she did me the favour of laughing. I carefully sidestepped the rocks on the bottom of the pond to walk closer to her, then flicked more water in her direction.

'No!' Katherine shrieked, but she made no move to run away as I walked out of the pond, grabbed her around the waist, and carried her into the water.

'Stefan! Stop!' she screamed as she clung to my neck. 'At least let me take off my dress!'

At that, I immediately let her go. She lifted her hands over her head, allowing me to easily pull off her dress. There she stood in her little white slip. I gaped in amazement. Of course I'd seen her body before, but it had always been in shadows and half-light. Now I saw the sun on her shoulders, and the way her stomach curved inward and I knew, for the millionth time, that I was in love.

Katherine dove underwater, re-emerging right next to me. 'And now, revenge!' She leaned down and splashed cool water on me with all her might.

'If you weren't so beautiful, I might fight back,' I said, pulling her towards me. I kissed her.

'The neighbours will talk,' she murmured against

my lips.

'Let them talk,' I whispered. 'I want everyone to know how much I love you.' She kissed me harder, with more passion than I'd ever felt. I sucked my breath in, feeling so much desire that I stepped away. I loved her so much that it almost hurt; it made it harder to breathe, harder to talk, harder to think. It was as if my desire was a force larger than myself, and I was simultaneously frightened and overjoyed to follow wherever it led me.

I took a shaky breath and looked up at the sky. Large thunderclouds had rolled in, obscuring the sky, which had been a pure cerulean just moments before. 'We should go,' I said, heading towards shore.

Sure enough, as soon as we stepped onto dry land, a clap of thunder rolled off in the distance.

'The storm came in fast,' Katherine observed as she wrung out her curls. She didn't seem at all self-conscious even though her soaking-wet white slip left nothing to the imagination. Somehow, it seemed almost more illicit and erotic to see her scantily dressed than to see her naked. 'One *could* think that it was almost a sign that our relationship is not meant to be.' Her voice was teasing, but I felt a shiver of dread go up my spine.

'No,' I said loudly, to reassure myself.

'I'm just teasing you!' she kissed my cheek before leaning down to pick up her dress. As she stole behind the weeping willow tree, I yanked up my breeches and put on my shirt.

She emerged from behind the tree a moment later, her cotton dress clinging to her curves, the damp tendrils of her hair sticking to her back. Her skin had a bluish quality to it.

I put my arms around her and rubbed her arms vigorously, trying to warm her up, though I knew that was impossible.

'I have something to tell you,' Katherine said as she tilted her face up to the open sky.

'What?' I asked.

'I would be honoured to attend the Founders Ball with you,' she said, and then, before I could kiss her again, she broke from my embrace and ran back to the carriage house.

CHAPTER

22

The week of the Founders Ball came with a cold spell that settled into Mystic Falls and refused to leave. Ladies walked around town in mid-afternoon in wool coats and shawls, and the evenings were cloudy and starless. Out in the field, workers fretted about an early frost. Still, that didn't stop people from as far away as Atlanta coming into town for the ball. The boarding-house was full, and the entire town had a carnival-like air in the days leading up to the event.

Damon was back at Veritas, his mysterious tenure with the brigade over. I hadn't told him that Katherine and I were attending the Founders Ball, and he hadn't asked. Instead, I'd busied myself with work, feeling renewed vigour about taking over Veritas. I wanted to prove to Father that I was serious about the estate and about growing up and assuming my place in the world. He'd been giving me more responsibility, allowing me to look over the ledgers and even encouraging me to go to Richmond with Robert to attend a livestock auction. I could see my life, ten years from now. I'd run Veritas, and Katherine would run our home, hosting parties and playing the occasional card game at night with Father.

The night of the ball, Alfred knocked on my door.

'Sir? Do you require any assistance?' he asked as I swung the door open.

I glanced at my reflection in the mirror. I was dressed in a black long-tailed coat and tie, with my hair slicked back. I looked older, more confident.

Alfred followed my gaze. 'Looking smart, sir,' he allowed.

'Thank you. I'm ready,' I said, my heart fluttering in excitement. Last night, Katherine had teased me mercilessly, not giving me any clues as to what she was going to wear. I couldn't wait to see her. I knew she'd be the most beautiful girl at the ball. More importantly, she was *mine*.

I headed down the stairs, relieved that Damon was nowhere to be found. I wondered whether he was attending the Founders Ball with some of his army friends or perhaps one of the town's girls. He'd been distant lately, impossible to find in the morning and at the tavern at night.

Outside, the horses were pawing at the drive. I entered the waiting coach, which clip-clopped its way to the carriage house.

I glanced out of the window, and noticed Katherine and Emily standing at the front door. Emily wore a simple black silk dress, but Katherine . . .

I had to press my back into the carriage seat to keep from jumping out of the moving coach. Her dress was emerald green, nipping in at the waist before flowing over her hips. The bodice was low and tight and showed off her creamy white skin, and her hair was pulled back on the top of her head, exposing her graceful, swan-like neck.

The second Alfred pulled back on the horses' reins, I opened the door of the coach and hopped out, smiling broadly as Katherine's eyes caught mine.

'Stefan!' she breathed, lifting her skirts slightly as she glided down the steps.

'Katherine.' I gently kissed her cheek before I offered my arm to her. Together, we turned and walked towards the carriage, where Alfred stood with the door open.

The road to Mystic Falls was filled with unfamiliar coaches of all shapes and sizes, leading to the Lockwood mansion on the far end of town. I felt a thrill of anticipation. This was the first time I'd ever escorted a girl to the Founders Ball. In all previous years, I'd spent most of the evenings playing poker with my friends. Invariably some sort of disaster happened. Last year, Matthew Hartnett had got drunk on whiskey and had accidentally unhitched the horses from his parents' coach, and two years ago, Nathan Layman had got into a fistfight with Grant Vanderbilt, and both ended up with broken noses.

We slowly made our way up to the mansion, finally reaching the front walk. Alfred stopped the horses and let us out. I laced my fingers with Katherine's, and together we walked through the open doors of the mansion and headed for the dining room.

The high-ceilinged room had been cleared of all furniture, and the candlelight lent a warm, mysterious glow to the walls. A band in the corner played Irish reels, and couples were already beginning to dance, even though the night was young. I squeezed Katherine's hand, and she smiled up at me.

'Stefan!' I whirled around and saw Mr and Mrs Cartwright. I dropped Katherine's hand immediately.

Mrs Cartwright's eyes were red, and she was positively gaunt compared to the last time I saw her. Meanwhile, Mr Cartwright seemed to have aged ten years. His hair was snow-white, and he was walking with the aid of a cane. Both wore purple sprigs of vervain – a tuft stuck out of Mr Cartwright's breast pocket, and the flowers were woven into Mrs Cartwright's hat – but other than that, they were clad entirely in black, for mourning.

'Mr and Mrs Cartwright,' I said, my stomach clenching with guilt. In truth, I'd nearly forgotten that Rosalyn and I had been engaged. 'It's good to see you.'

'You could have seen us sooner if you'd come to call on us,' Mr Cartwright said. He could barely hide the contempt in his voice when his gaze landed on Katherine. 'But I understand you must have been in deep . . . *grief* as well.'

'I will come now that I know you're taking visitors,' I said lamely, tugging at my collar, which suddenly felt quite tight around my neck.

'No need,' Mrs Cartwright said icily as she reached into her sleeve to pull out a handkerchief.

Katherine clasped Mrs Cartwright's hand. Mrs Cartwright looked down, an expression of shock on her face. A wave of apprehension ran through me, and I fought the urge to step between them and shield Katherine from their anger.

But then Katherine smiled, and amazingly, both Cartwrights smiled back. 'Mr and Mrs Cartwright. I am so sorry for your loss,' she said warmly, holding their gazes. 'I lost my parents during the Atlanta siege, and I know how hard it is. I didn't know Rosalyn well, but I do know she will *never* be forgotten.'

Mrs Cartwright blew her nose noisily, her eyes watering. 'Thank you, dear,' she said reverentially.

Mr Cartwright patted his wife on the back. 'Yes, thank you.' He turned to me, compassion replacing the scorn that had occupied his eyes just moments earlier. 'And please take care of Stefan. I know he's suffering.'

Katherine smiled as the couple rejoined the crowd.

I gaped in amazement. 'Did you compel them?' I asked, the word tasting bitter in my mouth.

'No!' Katherine placed her hand over her heart. 'That was good, old-fashioned kindness. Now, let's dance,' she said, tugging me over to the large ballroom. Luckily, the dance floor was a crush of bodies and the lighting was low, so it was almost impossible to make out specific people. Flower garlands hung from the ceiling, and the marble floor was waxed to a sheen. The air was hot and cloying with the scent of hundreds of competing perfumes.

I put my hand on Katherine's shoulder and tried to relax into the waltz. But I still felt jumpy. The conversation with the Cartwrights had stirred my conscience, making me feel vaguely disloyal to Rosalyn's memory, and to Damon. Had I betrayed him somehow by not telling him that Katherine and I were at the ball together? Was it wrong that I'd been grateful for his prolonged absences?

The band stopped, and as women adjusted their dresses and grasped their partners' hands again, I headed to the refreshment table in the corner.

'Are you all right, Stefan?' Katherine asked, gliding up beside me, worry lines creasing her lovely forehead.

I nodded, but I didn't break my stride. 'Just thirsty,' I lied.

'Me too.' She stood expectantly as I ladled the dark-red punch into a crystal tumbler.

I passed the glass to her and watched as she drank

deeply, wondering if that was what she looked like when she drank blood. When she placed the glass on the table, she had the slightest trace of red liquid around her mouth. I couldn't help it. With my index finger I wiped the drop off the side of her bow-shaped mouth. Then I put my finger in my own mouth. It tasted sweet and tangy.

'Are you sure you're all right?' Katherine asked.

'I'm worried about Damon,' I confessed as I poured myself a glass of punch.

'But why?' she asked, genuine confusion registering on her face.

'Because of you,' I said simply.

She took the tumbler from me and led me away from the refreshment table. 'He's like a brother to me,' she said, touching my brow with her icy fingers. 'I'm like his little sister. You know this.'

'But all those times when I was sick? When you and he were together? It seemed like . . .'

'It seemed like I needed a friend,' Katherine said firmly. 'Damon's a flirt. He doesn't want to be tied down, nor would I want to be tied to him. You are my love, and Damon is my brother.'

All around us, couples swirled in the semi-darkness, dipping in time to the music and laughing gaily at private jokes, seemingly without a care in the world. They, too, had to worry about attacks and the war and heartbreak, but they still laughed and danced. Why couldn't I as well? Why did I always have to doubt myself? I glanced at Katherine. A dark curl had come loose from her updo. I tucked it behind her ear, relishing the silky feel of the strands between my fingers. Longing coursed through me, and as I stared into her deep brown eyes, all feelings of guilt and unease vanished.

'Shall we dance?' she asked, taking my hand and pressing it to her cheek.

Through the crowded dance floor, I spotted Father, Mr Cartwright and the rest of the Founders whispering furiously in a far corner.

'No,' I whispered huskily. 'Let's go home.'

I grabbed Katherine's shoulder, and we whirled around the dance floor until we reached the kitchen, where servants were busily preparing refreshments. Hand in hand, we tore through the kitchen – much to the confusion of the servants – and exited at the back of the house.

We sprinted into the night, oblivious to the cold air, the shrieks of laughter from the mansion, and the fact that we'd just run out on the social event of the season.

The coach was tied near the Lockwoods' stable. Alfred was no doubt playing craps with the other servants.

'After you, my lady,' I said, lifting Katherine by the waist and placing her in the passenger seat. I hoisted myself up to the driver's seat and cracked the whip, which immediately caused the horses to start clip-clopping in the direction of home.

I grinned at her. We had an entire evening of

freedom in front of us, and it was intoxicating. No having to sneak into the carriage house. No skirting the servants. Just hours of uninterrupted bliss.

'I love you!' I yelled, but the wind stole the words as soon as they left my mouth. I imagined them travelling with the breeze, floating through the entire world until every person in every town knew of my love.

Katherine stood up in the coach, her curls whipping wildly around her face. 'I love you, too!' she shouted, and then collapsed into giggles on the seat.

By the time we got back to the carriage house, we were both sweaty and red-cheeked. The second we reached Katherine's chambers, I pulled the dress off her slim frame and, seized by my passion, gently ran my teeth against her neck.

'What are you doing?' She stepped back and stared at me sharply.

'I'm just . . .' What *was* I doing? Playacting? Trying to seem as if Katherine and I were the same? 'I guess I wanted to know how you feel when you . . .'

She bit her lip. 'Maybe someday you'll find out, my innocent, sweet Stefan.' She lay back on the bed, arranging her hair on the snow-white goose-down pillow. 'But right now, all I want is you.'

I lay down next to her, tracing the curve of her chin with my index finger as I put my lips to hers. The kiss was so soft and tender that I felt her essence and mine combine, creating a force that was larger than ourselves. We explored each other's bodies as if for the first time. In the dim light of her chambers, I was never sure where reality ended and my dreams began. There was no shame, no expectation, just passion and desire, and a sense of danger that was mysterious and beautiful and consuming.

That night, I would have allowed Katherine to consume me entirely and claim me for her own. I would have gladly offered up my neck if it meant that we could have stayed locked in that embrace for all eternity.

CHAPTER

23

That night, though, the embrace did end, and I fell into a black, dreamless sleep. But my mind and body jerked into sudden wakefulness when I heard a sharp clanging sound that seemed to reverberate through my limbs.

'Murderers!'

'Killers!'

'Demons!'

The words floated through the open window, chant-like. I crept to the window and creaked open the shutter. Outside, across the pond, there were flashes of fire, and I even heard the sound of rifles firing. Dark bodies moved en masse, like a swarm of locusts descending upon a cotton field.

'Vampires! Killers!'

I began to make out more and more words from

the angry roar of the crowd. There had to be at least fifty men in attendance. Fifty drunken, angry, murderous men. I grabbed Katherine's shoulder and began shaking her hard.

'Wake up!' I whispered urgently.

She sat up with a start. The whites of her eyes looked huge, and there were shadows beneath her eye sockets. 'What is it? Is everything OK?' Her fingers fluttered to her necklace.

'No, it's not OK,' I whispered. 'The brigade is out. They're searching for vampires. They're on the main road right now.' I pointed out of the window.

The yelling and shouts were getting closer. The fire blazed in the night, flames reaching towards the night sky like red daggers. Fear shot through me. This wasn't supposed to be happening – not yet.

Katherine slipped out of bed, tucking the white quilt around her body, and closed the shutters with a bang. 'Your father,' she said, her voice hard.

I shook my head. It *couldn't* be. 'The siege is set for next week, and Father is not the type to deviate from an established plan.'

'Stefan!' she said sharply. 'You promised you would do something. You *have* to stop this. These men don't know what they're fighting, and they *don't* know how dangerous this is. If they keep doing this, people will get hurt.'

'Dangerous?' I asked, rubbing my temple. I suddenly had a pounding headache. The shouting grew quieter now; it seemed the mob was pressing forward – or perhaps dispersing. I wondered if this was more a protest spurred by liquid courage than an actual siege.

'Not from me, but from whoever has launched these attacks.' Katherine's eyes met mine. 'If the townspeople know what's safe for them, what's *best* for them, they'd stop the hunt. They'd allow us to resolve things. They'd allow us to find the source of the attacks.'

I sat on the edge of the bed and rested my elbows against my knees, staring down at the worn wooden floorboards in dismay, as if I could find some sort of answer, some sort of way to stop what already seemed to be happening.

She took my face in her hands. 'I am entirely at your mercy. I need you to protect me. Please, Stefan.'

'I know, Katherine!' I said half-hysterically. 'But what if it's too late? They have the brigade, they have their suspicions, they even have an invention designed to find vampires.'

'What?' she reared back. 'An invention? You didn't tell me that,' she said, her voice taking on a note of accusation.

A hard lump settled in my chest as I explained Jonathan's device. How had I failed to mention it to Katherine? Would she ever forgive me?

'Jonathan Gilbert.' Her face twisted in contempt. 'So that fool thinks he can just hunt us down? Like animals?'

I recoiled. I'd never heard her use that harsh tone.

'I'm sorry,' she said in a more composed voice, as if she'd sensed the flicker of fear in my heart. 'I'm sorry. It's just . . . you simply can't imagine what it's like to be hunted.'

'The voices seem to be quieting.' I peeked through the shutters. The mob was indeed beginning to disperse, the flames becoming shaky dots in the inky black night. The danger was seemingly gone.

For now at least. But by next week, they'd have Jonathan's invention. They'd have a list of vampires. And they'd find every single last one of them.

'Thank goodness.' Katherine sank down onto the bed, pale as I'd ever seen her. A lone tear fell from her eye and trickled down her alabaster skin. I reached to wipe it away with my index finger, then gently touched my tongue to my skin, an echo of what I'd done at the Founders Ball. I sucked my finger, finding that her tears tasted salty. Human.

I pulled her to me, wrapping her in a tight embrace. I'm not sure how long we sat there, together. But as the faint light of the morning came through the windows I stood up.

'I will stop it, Katherine. I will protect you to the death. I swear it.'

CHAPTER
24

September 25, 1864
They say love can conquer all. But can it conquer
Father's belief that Katherine and those like her are
demons – devils? I do not exaggerate when I say
Katherine is an angel. She saved my life – and
Anna's. Father must know the truth. Once he does, he
will be unable to deny Katherine's goodness. It is my
duty as a Salvatore to stay true to my convictions and
to the ones I love.

Now is the time for action, not doubt. Confidence
courses through my veins. I will make Father
understand the truth – that we are all the same. And
with that truth will come love. Father will call off the
siege.

This I swear on my name and my life.

For the rest of the day, I sat at my desk in my bedroom, glancing at an empty notebook as I contemplated what to do. If Father knew Katherine was a vampire, he'd call off the hunt. He had to. I'd seen him laugh with her, attempt to impress her with stories of his boyish antics back in Italy and treat her as he'd have treated a daughter. Katherine gave my father a vigour I'd never seen in him. She gave my father life.

But how could I persuade him of this, when he so deeply despised demons? Then again, Father was rational. Logical. Maybe he could learn what Katherine had already taught me: that vampires weren't all evil. They walked among us, they cried human tears; all they wanted was a true home – and to be loved.

Finally, I steeled my courage and stood up, closing the notebook with an abrupt clap. This wasn't a schoolboy's assignment, and I didn't need notes to speak from my heart. I was ready to speak to Father man to man. After all, I was nearly eighteen, and he was planning to leave me Veritas.

I took a deep breath and walked down the winding staircase, through the quiet living room, and knocked sharply on the door to Father's study.

'Come in!' Father's muffled voice called. Before I had even put my hand on the knob, he swung the door open himself. He wore a tailored jacket, with a sprig of vervain in the lapel, but I noticed that instead of being clean shaven, he sported salt-and-pepper stubble and his eyes were bloodshot and hooded.

'I didn't see you last night at the ball,' Father said as he ushered me into his study. 'I hope you weren't part of that noisy, careless mob.'

'No.' I shook my head vigorously, feeling a flicker of hope. Did this mean he was no longer planning an attack?

'Good.' Father sat at his oak desk and slammed his leather-bound book shut. Beneath it, I could see complicated drawings and diagrams of the town, with X's over certain buildings, including the apothecary. And just like that, the flicker of hope was extinguished, and cold, hard fear took up residence in its place.

Father followed my gaze. 'As you can see, our plans are much more thought-out than that foolish brigade of drunks and boys. Luckily Sheriff Forbes and his team put a stop to them, and none of them will be welcome at our own siege.' He sighed and steepled his fingers together. 'We're living in dangerous and uncertain times, and your actions need to reflect that.' His dark eyes softened for a second. 'I just want to make sure your decisions, at least, are prudent.' He didn't add 'unlike Damon's', but he didn't have to. I knew that was what he was thinking.

'So the siege . . .'

'Will happen next week as planned.'

'What about the compass?' I asked, remembering the conversation with Katherine.

Father smiled. 'It works. Jonathan's been tinkering with it.'

'Oh.' A wave of horror rushed through me. If it worked, then that meant there was no doubt Father would find Katherine. 'How do you know that it works?'

He smiled and rolled up his papers. 'Because it does,' he said simply.

'Can I talk to you about something?' I asked, hoping my voice betrayed none of my nerves. An image of Katherine's face flashed in my head, giving me the strength to lock eyes with Father.

'Of course. Sit down, Stefan,' he commanded. I perched in the leather wingback chair near the bookshelves. He stood up and walked over to the decanter of brandy on the corner table. He poured a glass for himself, then one for me.

I took the tumbler and held it to my lips, taking a tiny, almost imperceptible sip of the liquid. Then I steeled my courage and stared straight at him. 'I have concerns about your plan for the vampires.'

'Oh? And why is that?' Father leaned back against his chair.

I nervously took a large gulp of brandy. 'We're making the assumption that they're as evil as they've been characterized. But what if that's not true?' I asked, willing myself to meet Father's gaze.

He snorted. 'Have you any evidence to the contrary?'

I shook my head. 'Of course not. But why take

what people say at face value? You taught us differently.'

Father sighed and walked to his decanter, pouring more brandy. 'Why? Because these creatures are from the darkest parts of hell. They know how to control your mind, seduce your spirit. They are deadly, and they need to be destroyed.'

I glanced down at the amber liquid in my glass. It was as dark and murky as my thoughts.

Father tipped his glass to me. 'I shouldn't have to tell you, son, that those who stand with them, those who bring shame to their families, will be destroyed as well.'

A chill went up my spine, but I held his gaze. 'Anyone who stands with evil should be destroyed. But I hardly think it's prudent to assume that all vampires are evil just because they happen to be vampires. You always taught us to see the good in people, to think for ourselves. The last thing this town needs, when there have already been so many deaths from the war, is more senseless killing,' I said, remembering Pearl and Anna's terrified expressions in the woods. 'The Founders need to rethink the plan. I'll come to the next meeting with you. I know I haven't been as involved as I could have been, but I'm ready to take on my responsibilities.'

Father sank back into his chair, leaning his head against the wooden back. He closed his eyes and massaged his temples. For several long moments he remained in that posture.

I waited, every muscle in my body coiled to receive the angry flurry of words that was sure to fly from his mouth. I stared dejectedly into my glass. I had failed. I had failed Katherine, Pearl and Anna. I had failed at securing my own happy future.

Finally, Father's eyes snapped open. To my surprise, he nodded. 'I suppose I could give the matter some thought.'

Cool relief flooded my body, as if I'd just jumped into the pond on a scorching summer day. He would give the matter some thought! To some, that might not seem to be much, but from my stubborn father, it meant everything. It meant there was a chance. A chance to stop sneaking around in the dark. A chance for Katherine to remain safe. For us to be together, forever.

Father lifted his glass to me. 'To family.'

'To family,' I echoed.

Then he drained the rest of his glass, which compelled me to do the same.

CHAPTER

25

Excitement coursed through my veins as I stole out of the house, across the dew-dropped lawn, and towards the carriage house. I slid past Emily, who held the door open for me, and bounded up the stairs. I no longer needed the candle to find my way to Katherine. There, in the bedroom, she was wearing her simple cotton nightdress and absentmindedly swinging a crystal necklace that sparkled in the moonlight.

'I think Father may be persuaded to call off the siege. At least he's willing to talk. I know I'll be able to change his mind,' I exclaimed, twirling her around the room.

I expected her to clap with glee, for her smile to mirror my own. But instead Katherine disengaged herself from my grip and placed the crystal necklace on her nightstand.

'I knew you were the man for the job,' she said, not looking at me.

'Better than Damon?' I asked, unable to resist.

Finally Katherine smiled. 'You need to stop comparing yourself to Damon.' She stepped closer to me and grazed my cheek with her lips. I shivered with pleasure as she pulled my body to hers. I held her tightly, feeling her back through the thin cotton of her nightdress.

She kissed my lips, then my jaw, running her lips, feather light, down the curve of my neck. I moaned and pulled her even closer, needing to feel all of her against all of me. Then she plunged her teeth into my neck. I let out a strangled gasp of pain and ecstasy as I felt her teeth inside my skin, felt her draw blood from me. It felt as though a thousand knives were piercing my neck. Still I held her more tightly, wanting to feel her mouth on my skin, wanting to fully submit myself to the pain that fed her.

Just as suddenly as she bit me, Katherine broke away, her dark eyes on fire, agony etched on her face. A small stream of blood trickled from the corner of her lip, and her mouth twisted in excruciating pain. 'Vervain,' she gasped, stepping backwards until she collapsed on the bed. 'What have you done?'

'Katherine!' I put my hands to her chest, my lips to her mouth, trying desperately to heal her the way she had healed me back in the forest. But she pushed me away, writhing on the bed, clutching her hands to her mouth. It was as if she were being tortured by an unseen hand. Tears of agony spilled from her eyes.

'Why did you do this?' Katherine clutched her throat and closed her eyes, her breath slowing into guttural gasps. Every anguished cry from her felt like a small stake in my own heart.

'I didn't! Father!' I shouted as the dizzying events of that evening occurred to me. My brandy. Father. He *knew*.

There was a clatter from downstairs, and then Father burst in.

'Vampire!' he roared, holding up a crudely-made stake. Katherine writhed on the floor in pain, shrieking in a high-pitched tone I'd never heard before.

'Father!' I shouted, holding my hands up as he used his boot to prod her. She moaned, her arms and legs kicking in opposite directions.

'Katherine!' I fell to my knees and held her body close in my arms. She shrieked, her eyes rolling back so all I could see was white. Foam appeared at the corners of her blood-caked lips, as though she were a rabid animal. I gaped in horror and let go, her body falling to the floor with a sickening thud.

I inched back, sitting on my heels and gazing at the ceiling as if in prayer. I couldn't face Katherine, and I couldn't face Father.

She let out another high-pitched wail as Father prodded her with his stake. She reared up – foaming at the mouth, her fangs bared, her eyes wild and unseeing – before falling back in a writhing pile.

Bile rose in my throat. Who was this monster?

'Get up.' Father dragged me to my feet. 'Don't you see, Stefan? Don't you see her true nature?'

I gazed down at Katherine. Her dark curls were matted to her forehead by sweat, her dark eyes were wide and bloodshot, her teeth were covered with foam, and her entire body was shaking. I didn't recognize any part of her.

'Go get Sheriff Forbes. Tell him we have a vampire.'

I stood transfixed in horror, unable to take a step in any direction. My head pounded, my thoughts whirled in a confused tangle. I loved Katherine. *Loved* her. Right? So why now did this . . . *creature* disgust me?

'I did not raise my sons to be weak,' Father roared, shoving a bundle of vervain in my shirt pocket. 'Now go!'

My breath came in deep rasps. The heat was suddenly stifling, unbearable. I couldn't breathe, couldn't think, couldn't do anything. All I knew was that I couldn't stand being in that room for one second longer. Without a backward glance at my father or at the vampire writhing on the floor, I rushed out of the house, taking the steps three at a time, and raced for the road.

CHAPTER

26

I cannot say how long I ran. The night was clear and cold, and my heart felt as though it were pounding in my neck, in my brain, in my feet. I occasionally pressed my hand to the wound on my neck, which was still bleeding. The area was warm to the touch, and I felt dizzy whenever I put my hand on it.

With each footstep, a new image appeared in my head: Katherine, bloodstained foam collecting at the corners of her mouth; Father, standing above her with a stake. Memories blurred, so I wasn't sure whether the red-eyed, shrieking monster who was on the floor was the same person who'd lunged at me with her teeth, who'd caressed me in the pond, who haunted my dreams and my waking hours. I shivered uncontrollably and lost my footing, tripping over a felled branch. I landed in the dirt, on my hands and knees, and retched repeatedly, until the iron-like taste in my mouth disappeared.

Katherine was about to die. Father hated me. I didn't know who I was, or what I should be doing. The entire world was turned upside down, and I felt dizzy and weak, sure that no matter what I did, I would cause destruction. This was all my fault. All of it. If I hadn't lied to Father and kept Katherine's secret . . .

I forced myself to catch my breath, then stood up and began running again.

As I ran, the scent of the vervain in my pocket filled my nostrils. Its sweet, earthy fragrance wafted through my body, seeming to clear my head and imbue my limbs with a wakeful energy. I turned left on the dirt path, surprised at the course I was choosing, but for the first time in weeks, I felt certain about my actions.

I burst into the sheriff's office, where Sheriff Forbes sat with his feet up on the desk, asleep. In the one holding cell, the town drunk, Jeremiah Black, was snoring loudly, obviously sleeping off a bad night at the saloon. Noah, a young officer, was also nodding off on a wooden chair outside the cell.

'Vampires! There are vampires at Veritas!' I yelled, causing Sheriff Forbes and Jeremiah to simultaneously snap to attention.

'Let's go. Follow me,' Sheriff Forbes said, grabbing a club and a musket. 'Noah!' he yelled. 'Get the wagon and follow behind with Stefan.'

'Yes, sir,' Noah said, jumping to his feet. He pulled a club from a hook on the wall and passed it to me. Just then, I heard a piercing noise, and I realized that Sheriff Forbes was ringing the alarm outside the sheriff's office. The bell clanged over and over again.

'I can help. Please?' Jeremiah slurred, both hands on the bars. Noah shook his head and hurriedly ran through the building, his boots echoing against the wooden floor beams. I followed him, stopping to watch as he hastily hitched two horses to a long iron wagon.

'Come on!' Noah called impatiently, holding his whip.

I jumped up onto the seat next to Noah and watched as he cracked the whip, causing the horses to gallop at breakneck speed down the hill and into town. People were standing outside their houses in nightclothes and rubbing their eyes, some hitching horses to wagons and coaches.

'Attack at the Salvatore estate!' Noah called, over and over again, until his voice almost broke. I knew I should help. But I couldn't. Instead, I felt fear grip my heart as the wind whipped my face. I heard the clip-clopping of horses in the distance, and saw doors being flung open and more townspeople in their nightclothes hastily grabbing rifles, bayonets and any other weapon they could find. As we galloped through town, I noticed the apothecary was closed tightly. Could Anna and Pearl be at home? If so, I needed to give them a warning.

No. The word came so strongly, it was as if my father had whispered it in my ear himself. I needed to make things right for me, for the Salvatore name. The only people I cared about were Father and Damon, and if anything happened to them . . .

'Attack at the Salvatore estate!' I yelled, my voice breaking.

'Attack at the Salvatore estate!' Noah repeated, his words sounding like a chant. I looked up at the sky. The moon was a tiny sliver, and clouds obscured any hint of starlight. But suddenly, as we rode up the hill, I saw Veritas lit up like morning, with a mob of what looked like a hundred people brandishing torches and standing on the steps of the porch, yelling.

Pastor Collins stood on the porch swing, calling out prayers, as several people watched him, kneeling on the ground and praying. Next to him was Honoria Fells, yelling to anyone who would listen about demons and repentance. Old Man Robinson was brandishing his torch and threatening to burn down the entire estate.

'Stefan!' Honoria called as I jumped off the wagon before it stopped. 'For your protection,' she said, proffering a branch of vervain.

'Excuse me,' I called hoarsely, as I pushed through the horde, using my elbows, and ran to the carriage house and up the stairs. I heard angry voices from the chambers.

'I will take her! We'll leave, and you won't see either of us again!' Damon's voice, as low and ominous as incoming thunder.

'Ungrateful!' Father roared, and I heard a sickening crack. I bounded up the stairs and saw Damon, slumped against the doorway, a trickle of blood oozing from his temple. The door had cracked from the impact of his body.

'Damon!' I called, falling onto my knees next to my brother. He tried to struggle to his feet. I winced as I saw the blood flooding from his temple. When he turned towards me, his eyes blazed with anger.

Father stood, stake in hand. 'Thank you for getting the sheriff, Stefan. You did the right thing. Unlike your brother.' Father reached out to him, and I gasped, sure he would hit him again. But instead he stretched out his hand. 'Stand up, Damon.'

Damon slapped away Father's hand. He stood on his own, wiping the blood from his head with the back of his hand.

'Damon. Listen to me,' Father continued, ignoring the look of pure hatred on Damon's face. 'You were bewitched by the demon . . . by that *Katherine*. But now she will disappear and you must side with what's right. I showed you mercy, but these people . . .' He gestured towards the window and the angry mob beyond it.

'Then let me be killed,' Damon hissed, as he stormed out of the door. He brushed past me, hitting me hard with his shoulder as he ran down the stairs.

From inside the room, an agonizing shriek emerged.

'Sheriff?' Father called, swinging open the door to Katherine's chambers. I gasped. There was Katherine, a leather muzzle over her face, her white arms and legs bound together.

'She's ready,' Sheriff said grimly. 'We'll take her to the wagon and add her to the list. Gilbert's got the compass and is rounding up the vampires in town. By daybreak, we will have rid the town of this scourge.'

Katherine stared at me, a desperate, pleading expression in her eyes. But what could I do? She was lost to me now.

I turned down the stairs and ran.

CHAPTER
27

I ran out onto the lawn. Fire was everywhere, and I noticed that the servants' quarters had burst into flames. Right now, the main house looked safe, but who knew how long that would last? I saw glimpses of flames in the woods, and a large group converged around the police wagon. But all I cared about was finding Damon. Finally, I spotted a figure wearing a blue coat, sprinting towards the pond. I turned on my heel and followed him through the field.

'Stefan!' I heard my name and stopped, looking about wildly. 'Over here!' I turned and saw Jonathan Gilbert, his eyes wild, standing at the edge of the forest, a bow and arrow in one hand, his compass in the other. Jonathan looked down at his invention almost in disbelief. 'There's a vampire in the forest. My compass is pointing, but I need help with a lookout.'

'Jonathan!' I yelled, panting. 'I can't . . . I have to find . . .'

Suddenly, I saw a flash of white from the forest. Jonathan turned and raised his bow to his shoulder. 'Who goes there?' he called, his voice ringing like a clarion bell. Instantly, he released the arrow. I saw the beginning of its arc as it pierced the darkness. Then we heard a scream, followed by a thud.

Jonathan ran into the forest, and I heard a long, low moan. 'Jonathan!' I called wildly, then stopped short. I saw him kneeling over a prone figure. He turned his head up to me, his eyes shining with tears.

'It's Pearl,' he said dully.

There was an arrow stuck under her shoulder. She moaned, and her eyes fluttered under her lids.

'Pearl!' Jonathan said, angrily this time, as he roughly yanked out the arrow. I turned in horror, not wanting to watch.

Instead, I ran with all my might towards the pond, hoping against hope that Damon was still there.

'Damon?' I called tentatively, as I picked my way around tree roots. My eyes took a moment to adjust to the wooded darkness and relative quiet of the forest. I saw a figure perched on a felled tree branch. 'Damon?' I called quietly.

The figure turned around, and I gasped. Damon's face was white, and his dark hair was sticking to his forehead. The gash at his temple was bordered by crusted blood, and the whites of his eyes were cloudy.

'You coward,' he hissed, drawing his knife from his pocket.

'No.' I held my hands up and took a step back. 'Don't hurt me.'

'Don't hurt me!' he mocked in a high-pitched voice. 'I knew you'd tell Father eventually. I just don't know why Katherine trusted you with her secret. Why she believed you wouldn't turn her in. Why she loved you.' His voice broke on the word *love*, and he dropped the knife. His face crumpled in anguish, and he didn't look dangerous or hateful. He looked broken.

'Damon, no. No. No.' I kept repeating the word as my mind whirled. Had Katherine loved me? I remembered the moments she'd stare at me, her hands on my shoulders. *You must love me, Stefan. Tell me we'll be together forever. You have my heart.* I'd always felt the same woozy, heady sensation running through my limbs and up to my brain, wanting to do anything for her. But now, when I thought of her true nature, all I could do was shudder. 'She didn't love me,' I said finally. She'd compelled me, and she made me hurt everyone I loved. I felt hatred rise up from the depth of my soul, and I wanted to lead the charge against Katherine.

Until I looked at my brother.

Damon rested his head in his hands, staring at the ground. It was then that I realized: Damon *loved* Katherine. He loved her despite, or maybe because of, her dark side. When I'd seen Katherine lying bound on the floor, foaming at the mouth, I'd felt a stomach-turning revulsion. But Damon's love for Katherine transcended her current state. He loved her so much that he'd accept the vampire side of her, instead of pretending it didn't exist. And in order to be truly happy, Damon needed to be with her. Now I understood. I needed to save Katherine to save Damon.

In the distance, wails and cries filled the gunpowder-scented air. 'Damon. Damon.' I repeated his name, each time with an increasing urgency. He looked up, and I saw tears in his eyes, threatening to spill out. Not since Mother died had I seen him cry.

'I'll help you save her. I know you love her. I will help.' I kept repeating the word *help*, as if it were some sort of charm. *Please*, I pleaded in my mind as I looked at Damon's eyes. There was a moment of silence. Finally, he offered an almost imperceptible nod.

'OK,' he said in a ragged voice, clasping my wrist and dragging me to the edge of the forest.

CHAPTER

28

'We need to act now,' Damon said when we reached the line of trees next to the field. The forest floor was slick with leaves, and there was no sound, not even of animals.

I'd spent the last minutes desperately racking my brain, trying to think of some way to save Katherine. But I couldn't. Our only hope was to enter the fray, say a prayer for Pearl and Anna, then focus on freeing Katherine. It would be incredibly dangerous. But there was no other way.

'Yes,' I replied with an authority I did not feel. 'Are you ready?' Without waiting for an answer, I deftly moved towards the forest border, guided by the faint sound of angry shouting. I could see the outline of the estate. Damon crept by my side. Suddenly I saw a large burst of flames erupt from the carriage house.

I gasped, but Damon simply glared at me.

Just then, I heard the strident voice of Jonathan Gilbert. 'Found another one!'

I crept closer to the edge of the forest, until I had a full view of Jonathan slamming Henry from the tavern against the back of the police wagon. Noah held one of his arms, while another guard I didn't recognize held the other one. Jonathan held out his compass, frowning.

'Stake him!' he said. The guard drew his bayonet back and thrust it into the centre of Henry's chest. Blood spurted as Henry shrieked into the night air. He slumped to his knees, his eyes wide and staring down at the bayonet lodged in his body. I turned towards Damon, both of us realizing that we didn't have any time to waste. Damon bit his lip, and I knew we were in this together. Even though we often acted differently, when it counted we thought the same way. Maybe *that* – the shorthand communication we had as brothers – would be what would save us, and would save Katherine.

'Vampires!' I yelled from the depths of the forest.

'We found one! Help!' Damon called.

Instantly, Noah and the other guard released their grip on Henry and ran towards us, their bayonets raised.

'Over there!' Damon panted, pointing deep into the forest as the two guards stepped closer. 'There was a man. We only saw a dark shadow, but he tried to attack my brother.' As if to illustrate his point,

Damon traced the sticky path of blood that had pooled onto my collarbone from my neck. I reached my own hand to that spot in surprise. I'd forgotten that Katherine had bitten me. It seemed like a lifetime ago.

The two guards looked at each other and nodded tersely. 'You boys shouldn't be out here without weapons. We've got some in the wagon,' Noah called, before charging into the forest.

'Good,' Damon said, almost under his breath. 'Let's go. And if you let me down, I'll kill you,' he said, breaking away towards the wagon. I followed him, moving wholly by adrenaline.

We reached the unguarded wagon. Low moans came from the inside. Damon kicked the back of the wagon open and leapt up to the platform. I followed, gagging when I entered. The scent of the wagon was acrid, a combination of blood and vervain and smoke. Bodies writhed in corners, but it was pitch-black, making it impossible to tell whether the figures were vampires or humans or a combination of the two.

'Katherine!' Damon hissed, leaning down and roughly touching each of the bodies in his search for her.

'Stefan?' a weak voice called from the corner, and I forced myself not to lash out, not to spit in the direction of the voice, not to stare into those villainous eyes and tell her I hoped she got exactly what she deserved. 'Damon?' the voice broke.

'Katherine. I'm here,' Damon whispered, making

his way towards the far end of the wagon. I continued to stand, as if glued to the spot. As my eyes adjusted to the dim light, I began seeing things that were more terrible than anything I'd ever seen in my worst dreams. On the floor of the wagon were almost a dozen bodies, some people I recognized from around town. Henry, a few regulars from the saloon and even Dr Janes. Some of the bodies had stakes in them, others had muzzles over their mouths, their hands and feet bound and their mouths seemingly frozen in wide O's of horror; some were simply curled up as if they were already dead.

The sight changed me, changed everything. I took off my hat and knelt down roughly, praying to God or whoever would listen to please save them. I remembered Anna's kitten-like cries, the dull fear in Pearl's eyes. Yes, they couldn't live here, but why did Father have to condone this brutal treatment? No one deserved to die like this, not even monsters. Why couldn't it be enough to simply run them out of town?

Damon knelt down, and I rushed over to his side. Katherine was lying on her back, ropes binding her arms and legs. The ropes must have been covered with vervain, because there were terrible burns on the patches of skin that touched the twine. A leather mask covered her face, and her hair was matted with dried blood.

I stood back, not wanting to touch her or even look at her, as Damon set to work untying the muzzle. Once she was free, I couldn't help but notice her teeth, her fangs, her true nature, obvious in a way I'd never seen before. But Damon was gazing at her as if in a trance. He gently brushed the hair off her face and slowly leaned in to kiss her lips.

'Thank you,' said Katherine simply. That was it. And watching them, the way her fingers stroked Damon's hair, the way he cried into her collarbone, I knew that this was true love. As they continued to gaze into each other's eyes, I pulled my knife out of my pocket and gently tried to cut the ropes that bound her. I worked slowly and carefully, knowing that any additional contact with the ropes would cause her even more pain.

'Hurry!' Damon whispered, sitting on his heels as he watched me work.

I freed one arm, then another. Katherine sighed shakily, shrugging her shoulders up and down as if to make sure they still worked.

'Help!' cried a pale, thin woman I didn't recognize. She was huddled in the very back of the wagon.

'We'll be back,' I said, lying through my teeth. We wouldn't be back. Damon and Katherine had to escape, and I had to . . . well, I had to help them.

'Stefan?' Katherine said weakly as she struggled to her feet. Damon instantly rushed to her side and supported her fragile body.

Just then, I heard footfalls near the wagon.

'Escape!' one of the guards called. 'We need backup. There's been a breach in the wagon!'

'Run!' I called, pushing Damon and Katherine in the opposite direction of the guard.

'No escape! All clear!' I shouted into the darkness, hoping that people would believe me as I hopped off the wagon.

I saw the explosion of gunpowder before I heard the shot. A loud wail rent the night air, followed quickly by another booming shot. Heart in my throat, I ran around the wagon, already knowing what I'd see.

'Damon!' I cried. He lay on the ground, blood oozing from his gut. Yanking off my shirt, I put the linen on the wound to stanch the bleeding. I knew it was no use, but still I held the fabric to his chest. 'Don't shut your eyes, brother. Stay with me.'

'No . . . Katherine. Save her . . .' Damon rasped, his head flopping towards the damp ground. I glanced, wild-eyed, from the truck to the woods. The two guards were sprinting back, Jonathan Gilbert behind them.

I stood up, and instantly my body was met with the explosive, piercing, agonizing hit of a bullet. I felt my chest exploding, felt the cool night air whoosh past my body as I fell back, onto my brother. I opened my eyes and looked up at the moon, and then everything faded to black.

CHAPTER

29

When I next opened my eyes, I knew I was dead. But this death wasn't the death of my nightmares, with black nothingness all around. Instead, I could smell the faraway scent of a fire, feel rough earth beneath my body, could feel my hands resting by my sides. I didn't feel pain. I didn't feel anything. The blackness enveloped me in a way that was almost comforting. Was this what hell was? If so, it was nothing like the horror and mayhem of last night. It was quiet, peaceful.

I tentatively moved my arm, surprised when my hand touched straw. I pushed myself up to a sitting position, surprised that I still had a body, surprised that nothing hurt. I looked around and realized that I wasn't suspended in nothingness. To my left were the rough-hewn slats of a wall of a dark shack. If I squinted, I could see sky between the cracks. I was *somewhere*, but where? My hand fluttered to my chest. I remembered the shot ringing out, the sound of my body thudding to the ground, the way I was prodded with boots and sticks. The way my heart had stopped beating and there had been a cheer that rose up before everything was quiet. I was dead. So then . . .

'Hello?' I called hoarsely.

'Stefan,' a woman's voice said. I felt a hand behind my back. I realized I was wearing a simple, faded blue cotton shirt and tan linen trousers, clothes I didn't recognize as my own. And though they were old, they were clean. I struggled to stand, but the small yet surprisingly strong hand held me down by my shoulder. 'You've had a long night.'

I blinked, and as my eyes adjusted to the light, I realized that the voice belonged to Emily.

'You're alive,' I said in wonderment.

She laughed, a low, lazy chuckle. 'I should be saying that to you. How are you feeling?' she asked, bringing a tin cup of water to my lips.

I drank, allowing the cool liquid to trickle down my throat. I'd never tasted anything so pure, so good. I touched my neck where Katherine had bitten me. It felt clean and smooth. I hastily yanked the shirt open, popping several buttons in the process. My chest was smooth, no hint of a bullet wound.

'Keep drinking,' Emily clucked in a way a mother might do to her child.

'Damon?' I asked roughly.

'He's out there.' Emily pointed her chin to the door. I followed her gaze outside, where I saw a shadowy figure sitting by the water's edge. 'He's recovering, just as you are.'

'But how . . .'

'Notice your ring.' Emily tapped my hand. On my ring finger was a gleaming lapis-lazuli stone, inset in silver. 'It's a remedy and a protection. Katherine had me make it for you the night she marked you.'

'Marked me,' I repeated dumbly, once again touching my neck, then allowing my fingers to drop to the smooth stone of the ring.

'Marked you to be like her. You're almost a vampire, Stefan. You're well into the transformation,' Emily said, as if she were a doctor diagnosing a patient with a terminal illness.

I nodded as if I understood what Emily was saying, even though it might as well have been a completely different language. Transformation?

'Who found me?' I asked, starting with the question I cared least about.

'I did. After the shots were fired on you and your brother, everyone ran. The house burned down. People died. Not just vampires.' Emily shook her head, her face deeply troubled. 'They brought all the vampires to the church and burned them there. Including her,' Emily said, her tone impossible to comprehend.

'Did she make me a vampire, then?' I asked,

touching my neck.

'Yes. But in order to complete the transition, you must feed. It's a choice you have to make. Katherine had the power of destruction and death, but even she had to allow her victims that choice.'

'She killed Rosalyn.' I knew it in the same way I'd known Damon loved Katherine. It was as if a cloud had lifted, only to reveal more blackness.

'She did,' Emily said, her face inscrutable. 'But that has nothing to do with what happens. If you choose, you can feed and complete the transition, or let yourself . . .'

'Die?'

Emily nodded.

I didn't *want* to feed. I didn't *want* Katherine's blood inside me. All I wanted was to go back several months, before I'd ever heard the name Katherine Pierce. My heart twisted in agony for all I'd lost. But there was someone who'd lost more.

As if she'd read my mind, Emily helped me to my feet. She was tiny, but strong. I stood up and shakily walked outside.

'Brother!' I called. Damon turned, his eyes shining. The water reflected the rising sun, and smoke billowed through the trees in the distance. But the clearing was eerily quiet and peaceful, harkening back to an earlier, simpler time.

Damon didn't answer. And before I even realized what I was doing, I walked to the edge of the water. Without bothering to take off my clothes, I dove in. I came up for air and breathed out, but my mind still felt dark and dirty.

Damon stared down at me from the water's edge. 'The church burned. Katherine was inside,' he said tonelessly.

'Yes.' I didn't feel satisfaction or sadness. I just felt deep, deep sorrow. For myself, for Damon, for Rosalyn, for everyone who'd gotten caught in this web of destruction. Father had been right. There were demons who walked the earth, and if you didn't fight them, then you became one.

'Do you know what we are?' Damon asked bitterly.

We locked eyes, and instantly I realized that I didn't want to live like Katherine. I didn't want to see the sunlight only with the aid of the ring on my finger. I didn't want to always gaze at a human's neck as if contemplating my next feeding. I didn't want to live forever.

I ducked down under the surface of the water and opened my eyes. The pond was dark and cool, just like the shack. If this was what death was, it wasn't bad. It was peaceful. Quiet. There was no passion, but also no danger.

I surfaced and pushed my hair off my face, my borrowed clothes hanging off my soaked limbs. Even though I knew what my fate was, I felt remarkably alive. 'Then I'll die.'

Damon nodded, his eyes dull and listless. 'There's no life without Katherine.'

I climbed out of the water and hugged my brother. His body felt warm, real. Damon briefly returned my embrace, then hugged his knees again, his gaze fixed on a spot far away from the water's edge.

'I want it done,' Damon said, standing up and walking farther away towards the quarry. I watched his retreating back, remembering the time when I was eight or nine that my father and I had gone buck hunting. It was right after my mother had died, and while Damon had immersed himself in schoolboy antics like gambling and riding horses, I'd clung to my father. One day, to cheer me up, Father took me to the woods with our rifles.

We'd spent over an hour tracking a buck. Father and I headed deeper and deeper into the forest, watching the animal's every move. Finally, we were in a spot where we saw the buck bowing down, eating from a berry bush.

'Shoot,' Father murmured, guiding my rifle over my shoulder. I trembled as I kept my eye on the deer and reached for the trigger. But at the moment I released the trigger, a baby deer scampered into the field. The buck sprinted away, and the bullet hit the fawn in the belly. Its wobbly legs crumpled beneath it, and it fell to the ground.

I'd run to try to help it, but Father had stopped me, holding on to my shoulder.

'Animals know when it's time to die. Let's at least allow it the peace to do it alone,' Father said, forcibly marching me away. I'd wailed, but he was relentless.

Now, watching Damon, I understood. Damon was the same way.

'Goodbye, brother,' I whispered.

CHAPTER
30

Though Damon wanted to die alone, I had unfinished business to attend to. I made my way from the quarry and began to walk back to the estate. The woods smelled like smoke, and the leaves were starting to turn. They crunched under the worn boots I had on my feet, and I remembered all the times Damon and I had played hide-and-seek as children. I wondered if he had any regrets, or if he felt as empty as I did. I wondered if we'd see each other in Heaven, being as we were.

I walked towards the house. The carriage house was charred and burned, its beams exposed like a skeleton. Several of the statues around the labyrinth were broken, and torches and debris littered the once-lush lawn. But the porch light at the main house was on, and a buggy stood at attention beneath the portico.

I walked around the back and heard voices coming from the porch. Immediately, I dove under the hedges. Hidden by the leaves, I crawled on my hands and knees against the wall until I came to the bay window that looked into the porch. Peering in, I made out the shadow of my father. A single candle cast weak beams of light around the room, and I noticed that Alfred wasn't in his normal spot sitting at the door, ready to instantly greet guests. I wondered if any of the servants had been killed.

'More brandy, Jonathan? Laced with vervain. Not that we need to worry anymore,' Father said, his words floating out of the door.

'Thank you, Giuseppe. And thank you for having me here. I realize you have much on your mind,' answered Jonathan sombrely, as he accepted the tumbler. I saw the concern etched on Jonathan's face, and my heart went out to him for the terrible truth he'd had to learn about Pearl.

'Yes. Thank you,' Father said, waving off the thought. 'But it's important that we end this sad chapter of our town's history. It is the one thing I want to do for my sons. After all, I do not want the Salvatore legacy to be that of demon sympathizers.' Father cleared his throat. 'So the battle of Willow Creek happened when a group of Union insurgents mounted an attack on the Confederate camp,' he began in his sonorous baritone voice, as if telling a story.

'And Stefan and Damon hid out in the woods to see if they could find any rogue soldiers, and at that point . . .' Jonathan continued.

'At that point they were tragically killed, just like the twenty-three other civilians who died for their country and their beliefs. It was a Confederate victory, but it came at the cost of innocent lives,' Father said, raising his voice as if to make himself believe the story he was weaving.

'Yes. And I'll speak with the Hagertys about creating a monument. Something to acknowledge this terrible period in our town's history,' Jonathan murmured.

I raised myself up on my knees, peeking through a spot at the corner of the window. I saw Father nodding in satisfaction, and cold seeped through my veins. So this was the legacy of my death – that I was killed by a band of degenerate soldiers. Now I knew I needed to speak to Father more than ever. He needed to hear the whole truth, to know that Damon and I weren't *sympathizers*, to know that the problem could have been cured without so much bloodshed and violence.

'But Giuseppe . . . ?' Jonathan asked, taking a long drink from his tumbler.

'Yes, Jonathan?'

'It *is* a triumphant moment in our town's history. The vampires are destroyed, and their bodies will turn to dust. We rid the town of the scourge, and thanks to the burning of the church, it will never come back. There were hard choices and heroism, but we won. That is your legacy,' Jonathan said as he slammed his ledger closed with a definitive thump.

Father nodded and drained his own tumbler, then stood up. 'Thank you,' he said, holding out his hand. I watched as the two men shook hands and then Jonathan disappeared into the shadows of the house. A moment later, I heard his carriage being hitched and the horses riding away. I crawled to the edge of the hedgerow. I stood up, my knees creaking, and walked through the door and into the house that was once mine.

CHAPTER
31

I crept through the house, cringing every time my foot hit a loose floorboard or a creaky corner. From the light at the far end of the house, I could tell Father had left the sitting room and was already in his study, no doubt writing down the record he and Jonathan had concocted in his own journal. I stood in the door frame and watched him for a moment. His hair was snow-white, and I saw age spots on his hands. Despite the lies I'd heard earlier, my heart went out to him. Here was a man who'd never known an easy life and who, after burying a wife, now had to bury two sons.

I took a step towards him, and Father's head jerked upwards.

'Dear God . . .' he said, dropping his pen to the floor with a clatter.

'Father,' I said, holding out my hands to him. He stood up, his eyes darting wildly.

'It's OK,' I said gently. 'I just want to talk with you.'

'You're dead, Stefan,' Father said slowly, still gaping at me.

I shook my head. 'Whatever you think of Damon and me, you have to know that we didn't betray you.'

The fear on Father's face abruptly turned to fury. 'You *did* betray me. Not only did you betray me, you betrayed the whole town. You *should* be dead, after the way you've shamed me.'

I watched him, anger rising up inside me. 'Even in our death, you feel only shame?' I asked. It was something Damon would say, and in a way, I felt his presence beside me. I was doing this for him. I was doing it for both of us, so that at least we'd die with truth on our side.

But Father was barely listening. Instead, he was staring at me. 'You're one of them now. Isn't that right, Stefan?' Father said, backing away from me, slowly, as if I were about to lunge and attack him.

'No. *No*. I'll never be one of them.' I shook my head, hoping against hope that Father would believe me.

'But you *are*. I watched you bleed and take your last breath. I left you for dead. And now I see you here. You are one of them,' Father said, his back now against the brick wall.

'You saw me get shot?' I asked in confusion. I remembered the voices. The chaos. *Vampire* being yelled over and over again in the darkness. Feeling Noah pull me off Damon. Everything fading to black.

'I pulled the trigger myself. I pulled it on you, and I pulled it on Damon. And apparently it wasn't enough,' Father said. 'Now I need to finish the job,' he said, his voice as cold as ice.

'You killed your own sons?' I asked, anger of my own coursing through my veins.

Father stepped towards me menacingly, and even though he thought I was a monster, I was the one who felt fear. 'You were both dead to me as soon as you sided with the vampires. And now, to come in here and ask forgiveness, as if what you did could be excused with an *I'm sorry*. No. No.' Father stepped away from his desk and walked over to me, his eyes still darting to the left and the right, except that now it was as if he were the hunter, rather than a hunted animal. 'You know, it's a blessing your mother died before she could see what a disgrace you've become.'

'I haven't turned yet. I don't *want* to. I came to say goodbye. I'm going to die, Father. You did what you set out to do. You killed me,' I said. Tears sprang from my eyes. 'It didn't have to be this way, Father. That's what you and Jonathan Gilbert should write in your false history, that it didn't have to be this way.'

'*This* is the way it has to be,' Father said, lunging for a cane that he kept in a large vase in the corner of the room. Swiftly, he broke it in two on the floor and held the long, jagged end out to me.

Quickly, without thinking, I sidestepped Father and yanked his free arm back, sending him tumbling sideways against the brick wall.

Father screamed in anguish as he hit the floor. And then I saw it. The stake was protruding from his stomach, blood spurting in all directions. I blanched, feeling my stomach rise to my chest and bile fill my throat.

'Father!' I rushed over to him and bent down. 'I didn't mean to. Father . . .' I gasped. I grabbed the stake and yanked it out of his abdomen. He shrieked, and immediately blood gushed like a geyser from the wound. I watched, horrified, but also entranced. The blood was so red, so deep, so beautiful. It was as if it were calling to me. It was as if I'd die that second if I didn't have the blood. And so, unbidden, I moved my hand to the wound and brought my cupped hand to my lips, tasting the liquid as it touched my gums, my tongue and my throat.

'Get away from me!' Father hoarsely whispered, pushing himself away until his entire back was pressed against the wall. He scratched my hand in an effort to bat it away from the wound, then slumped against the wall, his eyes closing.

'I . . .' I began, but then felt a shooting, stabbing pain in my mouth. It was worse than what I remembered about being shot. It was a feeling of tightness, followed by the sensation of a million needles sticking into my flesh.

'Get away . . .' Father breathed, covering his face with his hands as he struggled for air. I pulled my own hands from my mouth and ran my fingers over my teeth, which had become sharp and pointed. Then I realized: I was one of them now.

'Father, drink from me. I can save you!' I said urgently, reaching down and pulling him up to a sitting position against the wall. I took my wrist and brought it to my mouth, allowing my newly knife-sharp teeth to easily rip the skin. I flinched, then held the wound out towards Father, who backed away, blood continuing to gush from his wound.

'I can fix you. If you drink this blood, it will heal your wounds. Please?' I begged, looking into Father's eyes.

'I'd rather die,' he pronounced. A moment later his eyes fluttered shut and he slumped back on the floor, a pool of blood forming around his body. I placed my hand on his heart, feeling it slow until it stopped.

CHAPTER

32

I turned my back to the estate and began walking, then running, on the dirt road into town. Somehow, I felt that my feet barely touched the ground. I ran faster and faster, but my breath stayed the same. I felt that I could run like this forever, and I wanted to, because every step was taking me farther and farther away from the horrors I'd witnessed.

I tried not to think, tried to block the memories from my mind. Instead I focused on the light touch of the earth as I quickly placed one foot in front of the other. I noticed that even in the darkness, I could see the way the mist shimmered on the few leaves that still clung to the trees. I could hear the breath of squirrels and rabbits as they scampered through the forest. I smelled iron everywhere.

The dirt road changed into cobblestone as I

entered town. Getting to town seemed to have taken no time at all, though normally I traversed the same distance in no less than an hour. I slowed to a stop. My eyes stung as I glanced slowly from left to right. The town square looked *different* somehow. Insects crawled in the dirt between the cobblestones. Paint flaked off the walls of the Lockwood mansion, though it had been built only a few years ago. There was disrepair and decay in everything.

Most pervasive was the smell of vervain. It was *everywhere*. But instead of being vaguely pleasant, the scent was all-consuming and made me feel dizzy and nauseated. The only thing that countered the cloying scent was the heady smell of iron.

I inhaled deeply, suddenly knowing that the only remedy against the vervain-induced weakness was in that scent. Every fibre of my body screamed that I *had* to find the source of it, had to nourish myself. I looked around, hungrily, my eyes rapidly scanning from the saloon down the street to the market at the end of the block. Nothing.

I sniffed the air again, and realized that the scent – the glorious, awful, damning scent – was coming closer. I whirled around and sucked in my breath as I saw Alice, the pretty young barmaid from the tavern, walking down the street. She was humming to herself and walking unevenly, no doubt because she'd sampled some of the whiskey she'd been serving all night. Her hair was a red flame against her pale skin. She smelled warm and sweet, like iron and wood smoke and tobacco.

She was the remedy.

I stole into the shadows of the trees that flanked the street. I was shocked by how loud she was. Her humming, her breathing, each uneven footfall registered in my ear, and I couldn't help but wonder why she wasn't waking up everyone in town.

Finally, she passed by, her curves close enough to touch. I reached out, grabbing her by her hips. She gasped.

'Alice,' I said, my voice echoing hollowly in my ears. 'It's Stefan.'

'Stefan *Salvatore*?' she said, her puzzlement quickly turning to fear. She trembled. 'B-but you're dead.'

I could smell the whiskey on her breath, could see her pale neck, with blue veins running beneath her skin, and practically swooned. But I didn't touch her with my teeth. Not yet. I savoured the feeling of her in my arms, the sweet relief that what I'd spent the last moments insatiably craving was right in my hands.

'Shhh . . .' I murmured. 'Everything will be all right.'

I allowed my lips to graze her white skin, marvelling at how sweet and fragrant it was. The anticipation was exquisite. Then, when I couldn't take it any more, I curled my lips and plunged my teeth into her neck. Her blood rushed against my teeth, my gums, spurting into my body, bringing with it warmth and strength and *life*. I sucked hungrily, pausing only when Alice went limp in my arms and her heartbeat slowed to a dull thud. I wiped my mouth and looked down at her unconscious body, admiring my handiwork: two neat holes in her neck, just an inch or so in diameter.

She wasn't dead yet, but I knew she would be soon.

I slung Alice over my shoulder, barely feeling the weight and barely feeling my feet hit the ground as I ran through town, into the woods, and back to the quarry.

CHAPTER

33

Pale moonlight danced over Alice's bright hair as I rushed towards the shack. I ran my tongue over my still-sharp fangs, reliving the sensation of my teeth pressing into her pliant, yielding neck.

'You're a monster,' a voice somewhere in my mind whispered. But in the cloak of darkness, with Alice's blood coursing through my veins, the words held no meaning and were accompanied by no sting of guilt.

I burst into the shack. It was quiet, but the fire was well-tended and burned brightly. I watched the flames, momentarily entranced by the violets, blacks, blues and even greens within. Then I heard a faint breath in the corner of the room.

'Damon?' I called, my voice echoing so loudly against the rough-hewn beams that I winced. I was still in hunting mode.

'Brother?'

I made out a figure hunched under a blanket. I observed Damon from a distance, as if I were a stranger. His dark hair was matted to his neck, and he had streaks of grime along his face. His lips were chapped, his eyes bloodshot. The air around him smelled acrid – like death.

'Get up!' I said roughly, dropping Alice to the ground. Her almost-lifeless body fell heavily. Her red hair was matted with blood, and her eyes were half closed. Blood pooled around the two neat holes where I'd bitten her. I licked my lips but forced myself to leave the rest of her for Damon.

'What? What have you . . .' Damon's gaze shifted from Alice to me, then back to Alice. 'You fed?' he asked, shrinking even farther into the corner and covering his eyes with his hands, as if he could somehow erase the image.

'I brought her for you. Damon, you need to drink,' I urged, kneeling down next to him.

Damon shook his head. 'No. No,' he rasped, his breath laboured as he drew nearer to death.

'Just put your lips to her neck. It's easy,' I coaxed.

'I won't do it, brother. Take her away,' he said, leaning against the wall and closing his eyes.

I shook my head, already feeling a gnawing hunger in my belly. 'Damon, listen to me. Katherine is gone, but you're _alive_. Watch me. Watch how simple it is,' I said as I carefully found the original wound I had made on Alice's neck. I sunk my teeth back into the holes and drank. The blood was cold, but still it sated me. I looked up at Damon, not bothering to wipe the blood away from my mouth. 'Drink,' I urged, pulling Alice's body along the floor so it was lying next to him. I grabbed his back and forced him towards her body. He started to fight, then stopped, his eyes transfixed on the wound. I smiled, knowing how badly he wanted it, how he could smell the overpowering scent of desire.

'Don't fight it.' I pushed his back so that his lips were mere inches from the blood and held him there. I felt him take a deep breath, and I knew he was already regaining strength, just from seeing the red richness, the possibility of the blood. 'It's just us now. Forever. Brothers. There will be other Katherines, forever, for eternity. We can take on the world as we are.' I stopped, following Damon's gaze toward Alice's neck. Then he lunged and took a long, deep drink.

CHAPTER
34

I watched in satisfaction as Damon lustily drank, his tentative sips becoming gulps as he held his face down to Alice's neck. As her nearly lifeless body grew white, a healthy flush rose in Damon's cheeks.

As Damon drank the last drops of Alice's blood, I took a few steps outside the shack. I glanced around in wonder. Just last night, the area had seemed desolate, but now I realized that it teemed with life – the scent of animals in the forest, the flap of birds overhead, the sound of Damon's and my heartbeats. This spot – this whole world – was full of possibility.

My ring glimmered in the moonlight, and I brought it to my lips. Katherine had given me eternal life. Father always had told us to find our power, to find our place in the world. And I had, though Father hadn't been able to accept it.

I took a deep breath, and the coppery scent of blood filled my nostrils. I turned as Damon stepped out from the shack. He seemed taller and stronger than even a few moments ago. I noticed that he had a matching ring on his middle finger.

'How do you feel?' I asked, waiting for him to see everything I saw.

Damon turned away from me and walked towards the water. He knelt down and cupped the liquid to his mouth, washing away the remnants of blood on his lips.

I crouched next to him at the edge of the pond.

'Isn't it amazing? It's a whole new world, and it's ours. Forever!' I said, giddy. Damon and I would never have to grow older. Never have to die.

'You're right,' he said slowly, as if he were speaking in an unfamiliar language.

'We'll explore it together. Just think. We can go to Europe, explore the world, get away from Virginia and memories . . .' I touched his shoulder.

Damon turned to face me, his eyes wide. I stepped back, suddenly fearful. There was something different about him, a foreignness in his dark eyes.

'Are you happy now, *brother*?' he snorted derisively.

I took a step towards him. 'You'd rather be dead than have this whole world for the taking? You should be *thanking* me!'

Fury flashed in his eyes. 'Thanking you? I *never* asked you to make my life a hell from which I can't escape,' he said, spitting each word into the pond. Suddenly he pulled me into a hug with such strength that I gasped. 'But hear this, brother,' he hissed in my ear. 'Though we will be together for an eternity, I will make an eternity of misery for you.' With that, he released me from his grip and sprinted into the dark forest.

As his form disappeared into the black shadows of the trees, a single crow rose from the woods. It let out a plaintive shriek, and then it was gone.

Suddenly, in a world that mere moments ago had teemed with possibility, I was utterly alone.

EPILOGUE

October 1864

When I try to reconstruct that moment when I succumbed to my Power and destroyed my relationship with Damon, I imagine a split second of silence. In that second, Damon turned around, our eyes connected and we made peace.

But there was no silence, nor would there ever be again. Now I constantly hear the rustling of animals in the forest, the quickening of breath that occurs when any being knows danger is near, the pitter-patter-pause of a heart stopping. I also hear my thoughts, tumbling and colliding against each other like ocean waves.

If only I hadn't been weak when Katherine stared into my eyes. If only I hadn't gone back to see Father. If only I hadn't made Damon drink.

But I did. The fallout of those choices is a mantle that only grows darker and more nuanced with age. And I must live with the consequences of my misdeeds for eternity.

LUSTING AFTER MORE OF
STEFAN'S DIARIES?

TURN THE PAGE FOR A
SNEAK PEEK OF
BLOODLUST,
COMING JANUARY 2011.

CHAPTER

1

It was October. The leaves on the trees in the cemetery had turned a decayed brown, and a cold breeze had whistled in, replacing the stifling heat of Virginia summer. Not that I much felt it. As a vampire, the only temperature my body registered was that of the hot blood from my latest victim coiling through my veins.

I stood beneath the limbs of a large oak, a light mist swirling around my ankles, my shirt and hands sticky with the fresh blood of the girl I carried in my arms. My brother, Damon, lay prone at the base of the tree, his black eyes staring blankly up at me.

It had been days since I'd last forced him to feed. His body had taken on a chalky texture, blood vessels twisting darkly under his skin like cracks. Even now, as I dropped the nearly dead girl at his feet, I had to drape his right arm across her stomach to keep him from rolling over onto his back. Were it not for the blood that had purpled her dress, they would have looked like two lovers holding each other.

'I hate you with everything I am,' he whispered into her ear, though I knew his words were meant for me. She stirred but didn't open her eyes.

'You need your strength,' I said. 'Drink.'

He breathed in and his shoulders went limp. The metallic scent of her blood hung heavy in the air around us.

'That isn't strength,' he said, his eyes fluttering shut. 'It's weakness.'

'Stefan . . .'

This from the girl, Clementine Haverford, who reached a trembling hand out to me, her own sweet blood glistening like a silk glove around her fingers. Last summer, Clementine and I had kissed in the shadows of the Wickery Bridge after one of the games Damon had dreamed up for us. She'd allowed my hand to graze the bodice of her blue muslin dress. I kneeled down and tucked a few loose strands of hair behind her ear. A voice somewhere in my mind told me that I should feel regret over taking her life, but I felt nothing.

'You're a monster,' Damon said, keeping his lips as far as possible from the blood that seeped from Clementine's neck.

'Forever is a long time to deny what you are,' I told him.

From where we crouched in the hemlock grove, I could see my old neighbours milling around stone grave markers in the very centre of the cemetery. My heightened vampire senses allowed me to pick through the crowd of townspeople. Honoria Fells sniffed into a lace handkerchief. Sheriff Forbes kept his hand on his holster. Jonathan Gilbert cleared his throat and flicked open a pocket watch. My head throbbed with every whisper, like the world was breathing secrets directly into my eardrums.

Mayor Lockwood stood separate from the others, eulogizing our father, Giuseppe Salvatore – the man who had killed me and Damon, his only family, in cold blood. Father believed vampires to be utterly, unredeemably evil, and so he condemned us to death for trying to save Katherine Pierce, the vampire with whom we'd both fallen in love – the vampire who'd changed us to be like her.

Lockwood's voice sliced through the raindrops that had just begun to fall. 'We come together today to say farewell to one of Mystic Falls' greatest sons, Giuseppe Salvatore, a man for whom town and family always came before self.'

They stood before a gaping hole in the earth. Father would be wearing the suit he wore to church on Sundays, the black one, with the wide lapels that came together just at the point where I'd accidentally cut him open when he came at me with a stake. I could just make out the winged figure above him, the angel statue that marked my mother's final resting place. Two empty plots lay just beyond, where Damon and I should have been buried.

'It shan't be possible to picture this hero's life,' Lockwood continued, 'but in a portrait in which Giuseppe is flanked by his two fallen sons, heroes of the Battle of Willow Creek.'

Damon let out a low, rattling scoff. 'The portrait he paints,' he muttered, 'should contain the muzzle flash of Father's rifle.' He rubbed the place where Father's bullet had ripped through his chest only a week earlier.

Mayor Lockwood looked out over his congregation. 'A menace has descended on Mystic Falls, and only a brave few have risen to the challenge of protecting all that we hold dear. Jonathan, Giuseppe and I stood shoulder to shoulder against the threat. Now we must heed Giuseppe's last words as a call to arms.'

Lockwood's voice dragged with it the scent of smoky, blackened wood from the destroyed church on the opposite side of the cemetery. He was talking, ostensibly, about the groups of Union and Confederate soldiers who had been nipping about our part of Virginia for months, but there was no mistaking that he really meant vampires. Vampires like the ones Damon and I had been shot for trying to free, like the ones Damon and I had become.

'I could do it,' I told Damon. 'I could run out there and tear out all their throats before they knew it.'

'What's stopping you, brother?' he hissed. I knew his encouragement came only from the possibility of me dying in the act.

I held my breath and listened to Damon's panting, to the droning lies rising from Father's plot and to some kind of clicking, like a watch or a fingernail tapping against a mausoleum wall. I wasn't used to the rawness of my senses; the world gave me so much more as a vampire than it had as a human.

'Come,' I said, putting an arm around him. 'Let's get one last look at Mystic Falls' finest citizens.'

He didn't say anything but leaned into me, allowing me to hold him up as we moved from Clementine's bleeding body towards the grave site. We were just at a mausoleum a hundred yards from Father's grave when Lockwood introduced Gilbert to recite a prayer.

Gilbert licked his lips. As he read some prayer or another out loud, I noticed the clicking once more. It picked up in speed as we neared the crowd.

The clicking was now a steady, insistent rattle – and it seemed to be coming directly from Jonathan's hand. Then, with the angel wings marking mother's resting place stretched wide behind him, Jonathan Gilbert consulted the clicking object in his palm.

My blood ran cold. *The compass.* Jonathan had created a compass that, rather than pointing north, identified vampires.

Suddenly, Jonathan looked up. His eyes locked on Damon and me instantly.

'Demon!' He let out an unholy shriek and pointed in our direction.

'I think he means us, brother,' Damon said with a short laugh.

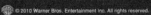

the Vampire Diaries

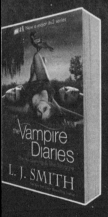

Sisters Red

'The wolf opened its long jaws, rows of teeth stretching for her. A thought locked itself in Scarlett's mind: I am the only one left to fight, so now, I must kill you ...'

An action-packed, paranormal thriller in a gritty urban setting, with a charming love story and unexpected twist that leaves you wanting more!

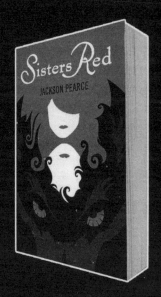

The Last Vampire

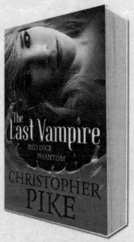
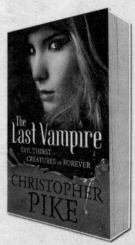

Alisa Perne is The Last Vampire. Beautiful, strong
deadly – and five thousand years old …

Volumes 1 – 3
OUT NOW

THE SECRET CIRCLE

THE INITIATION AND THE CAPTIVE PART I

Cassie is not happy about moving from sunny California to gloomy New England. She longs for her old life, her old friends … But when she starts to form a bond with a clique of terrifying but seductive teenagers at her new school, she thinks maybe she could fit in after all …

Initiated into the Secret Circle, she is pulled along by the deadly and intoxicating thrill of this powerful and gifted coven. But then she falls in love, and has a daunting choice to make. She must resist temptation or risk dark forces to get what she wants.

NIGHT WORLD

Volume 1
Books 1-3
OUT NOW

Secret Vampire
Poppy is dying, and it seems that James is her only chance of survival ... but is the price too high?

Daughters of Darkness
Mary Lynette has just met three mysterious sisters – on the run from their cruel brother. But can she protect them or herself with another threat lurking nearby?

Enchantress
Blaise is irresistible ... and deadly, but the Night World has rules, and Blaise is breaking them all ...

www.bookswithbite.co.uk
Sign up to the mailing list to find out about the latest releases from L.J. Smith

Remember
VOLUME ONE
Me

Don't be afraid ... be terrified.

Shari just stepped onto the
balcony for some fresh air, she
didn't mean to fall. Whilst her
friends assume it was suicide, she
knows otherwise, and now her
restless spirit must find the real
killer by any means possible ...

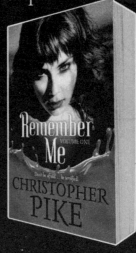